Mistletoe & Ivy

By

Ellen Dugan

Mistletoe & Ivy

Cover art designed by Kyle Hallemeier
Cover Image: fotolia: GaidenkoElena
Legacy Of Magick Logo designed by Kyle Hallemeier
Editing by Ana Blake
Copy Editing and Formatting by Libris in CAPS

Published by Ellen Dugan

Other titles by Ellen Dugan

THE LEGACY OF MAGICK SERIES

Legacy Of Magick, Book 1

Secret Of The Rose, Book 2

Message Of The Crow, Book 3

Beneath An Ivy Moon, Book 4

Under The Holly Moon, Book 5

The Hidden Legacy, Book 6

Spells Of The Heart, Book 7

Sugarplums, Spells & Silver Bells, Book 8

Magick & Magnolias, Book 9

Mistletoe & Ivy, Book 10

Cakepops, Charms & Do No Harm, Book 11
(Coming 2021)

THE GYPSY CHRONICLES

Gypsy At Heart, Book 1

Gypsy Spirit, Book 2

DAUGHTERS OF MIDNIGHT SERIES

Midnight Gardens, Book 1

Midnight Masquerade, Book 2

Midnight Prophecy, Book 3

Midnight Star, Book 4

Midnight Secrets, Book 5

Midnight Destiny, Book 6 (Coming Fall 2020)

HEMLOCK HOLLOW TRILOGY

Hemlock Lane (Coming 2020)

ACKNOWLEDGMENTS

As always, thanks to my beta readers and editors.

A special thanks to the friends and family who listened while I climbed my way out of the rabbit hole and back on track with book ten in the series.

The character of Ivy Bishop always manages to keep me on my toes.

She definitely had her mind made up when it came to finding her very own happy ever after.

Happy Reading and Happy Holidays!

DEDICATION

To my granddaughter, Kenzie.

You've brought such magick into the world for our entire family, little one.

We love you very much!

Mistletoe. I surmount all obstacles.

-Vanessa Diffenbaugh, *The Language of Flowers*

To me, the magic of photography, per se, is that you can capture an instant of a second that couldn't exist before and couldn't exist after.

-Mario Testin

CHAPTER ONE

I sat behind the counter of *Enchantments*, staring out the front window. The shop smelled cozily of cinnamon and vanilla. Holiday music played over the speakers in the store, white lights twinkled on both the tree displayed in the front window and in the pine garlands that swooped around the walls. It was all picture perfect, inviting and charming.

And I, Ivy Bishop, was bored out of my mind.

If you imagined that working in an occult store would be exciting...You'd be wrong. It was retail and, more often than not, we had looky-loos and tourists shopping in our store. The serious practitioners came in with a list, quickly made their choices, and got out.

There were three customers in the store at the moment. Two were thumbing through the books, and the third, a high school age girl, was selecting mini taper candles. She was placing them so carefully in her shopping basket that it made me wonder if she thought the fate of the world depended on her candle color choices.

Had to be a new practitioner, I decided.

My intuition was right on the money—as usual. Because not only did she purchase the candles, she also bought a 101 type of candle magick book.

Can I call 'em or what? I smiled to myself, rang her up, and she left the shop all smiles.

I perked up a bit when I noticed the young couple standing by the bookcase. They appeared to be in the throes of an argument.

What were they arguing about? I wondered, and my imagination bounced as I considered the possibilities. Perhaps one of them had massive gambling debts, or the other was a closeted Witch, and now their partner had just figured it out.

As they moved past the front counter, I caught their words, and was disappointed to discover that they were quarreling over which movie to go see tonight. The door closed behind them, leaving me alone in the shop.

I blew out a long, bored breath. *I needed to get out and do something exciting,* I decided. *Go have an adventure, or get laid.*

Sadly, none of those things were in my foreseeable future.

I'd been single for the last six months. Nathan Pogue and I had hit a sort of friendly impasse with our relationship. In May, when I'd received my bachelor's in photography, Nathan had gotten his master's degree in archaeology.

I wasn't surprised when he'd been offered a job back in Massachusetts, close to where his family lived. I'd figured it was coming—call me an intuitive. Nathan had been excited about the opportunity, and I'd been happy for him.

As for me, I'd only started working as a part-time assistant to a local wedding photographer, and I needed at least another year under my belt before I could go solo with my photography career.

Besides, I belonged in William's Ford. I knew it like I knew my own name. I couldn't relocate, and so my college romance came to a close. I'd been a little sad, but it wasn't like a gothic tragedy or anything. It was more of an inevitable thing.

When the time had come for Nathan to go, I'd helped him pack up his belongings and sent him off with a hug and a kiss. He promised he'd call me once he was home and settled. We said all the right things, the *kind* things. Sure, we'd keep in touch, maybe I'd fly out and spend a few weeks with him over the summer. That sort of thing. But I knew, down in my gut, that it wouldn't happen.

Nathan Pogue had *not* been the love of my life. He'd make some lucky woman very happy someday. But that woman wasn't me. Was I heartbroken? No. He'd been a great friend and lover for the past couple of years, but at our core we were simply too different. Nathan's family were all extremely private about their Craft. Their tradition was secret, as in they never discussed it with non-believers. Nathan had always been very serious and *very discreet* when it came to magick, while I was...

My thoughts trailed off as I caught my

reflection in the store mirror. Well, one thing was for certain. I've never been accused of being subtle.

I looked like what I was. A twenty-something Witch who had a love affair with gothic style fashion. I studied my image in the mirror, skimmed a hand through my long brown bob, and noticed a wayward smudge at the outer corner of my eye. With care, I wiped it away.

My affection for cosmetics was real and I still dramatically played up my green eyes for all they were worth. My days of vampire red, midnight black, or crazy blue streaked hair were gone, but not forgotten. These days I embraced my natural brown hair color. Ended up that it made my eyes all the more noticeable.

The long red and black buffalo plaid shirt I currently wore was cut like a duster. It skimmed my hips in the front, yet swung to my knees in the back. I'd layered it over a midnight scoop neck tee which framed my pentagram necklace and silver crescent pendant nicely. My leggings resembled leather—they weren't—and those were tucked into my over-the-knee black suede boots. It was a bohemian outfit, seasonal, with a dash of gothic flair, and yet still comfortable.

These days, when I was working on a wedding shoot I toned down my makeup and stuck to classic black slacks, simple blouses and blazers. It made me look more professional, even though I was more likely to be schlepping around equipment and getting folks into position for group shots as the 'assistant', rather than doing the main photos.

If I was lucky, sometimes I got the chance to take candid photos of the wedding party on my own. But still, every time I went with Jillian, I learned something new. She was a hell of a photographer, and I was lucky to have the opportunity to work with her.

I had even snagged a few clients of my own very recently. I had an outdoor engagement photo shoot booked for Thursday morning at a local Christmas tree farm. It was a clever idea, and a festive one. I planned to go scout out their chosen location on Wednesday, which would ensure that I'd capture the best photos with a minimum of fuss.

Alas, today I was working at the store because I'd volunteered to cover for Terry, our store manager. Which had given her the day off. Since the weekends were typically crazy busy on Main Street between Thanksgiving and Christmas, she appreciated the down time.

Drumming my fingertips on the counter, I considered what I could do with myself when I returned home. *I could always rent a movie, or work on finishing up my new apartment in the attic of the manor. I could go crazy and shop for the perfect accessories for my black and white bathroom. Or update my website for my photography business...*

Yes, my life had truly become that freaking exciting. It was a Monday afternoon during the first week of December, and there wasn't a lot happening in William's Ford.

With a sigh I gazed out the front window and told myself to enjoy the quiet. "Otherwise," I muttered, "I'm gonna end up like the old biddies in town." Determinedly, I went to the Yule tree in the front window to make a few adjustments to the ornaments.

The shop door opened. "Ivy!" Sharon Waterman greeted me. "How are you, dear?"

Sharon Waterman was in her sixties. She was

the head of the local Chamber of Commerce, a cheerful busy-body, and a hell of a lot of fun. "Hello Mrs. Waterman."

She headed straight for the candle display and picked up a few scented pillar candles. "Have you heard the latest news, dear?" And she was off.

The hot gossip around town since Thanksgiving weekend had been about the wild animal attack on a boy, I was informed. He'd been on a camping trip in the local woods, and speculation on what sort of animal had attacked him was running rampant.

"Oh," I said. "I'm sorry to hear about that. I hope he'll be okay."

Mrs. Waterman continued to fill me in as I rang her up. "I heard he's expected to make a full recovery," she said. "However, the four boys involved are all claiming that it was a *monster* that attacked them."

"You're kidding. A monster?" I'd said, handing her the shopping receipt. The woman had a nose for news, but there wasn't a mean bone in her body.

"Yes. A *monster.* Not since December of '79

has there been a sighting of that creature in the woods." Sharon Waterman paused, straightening her red scarf. "My father was never taken seriously, you know. And he'd even managed to get a few photographs of the beast after his own narrow escape!"

"Beast?" I grinned at her enthusiasm. "A local version of Bigfoot, no doubt?"

"There will always be skeptics, dear." Sharon sniffed, adjusting the sleeve of her navy winter coat. "My father swore that it was no Bigfoot. He'd always told me what he'd seen was *not of this world*."

It was everything I had not to giggle. Sharon Waterman was so damn much fun.

"But unfortunately," she continued, "since those naughty young men had all been drinking beer, most folks 'round here assume they were drunk, and figure it's all a teenage prank."

"Teenage boys drinking beer in the woods?" I laughed. "What are the odds?"

"I hope this doesn't all start up again," she said, tucking her wallet back in her purse. "Those poor boys. You take care, now." Mrs. Waterman gave me a wave and left.

I went to go straighten the candles she'd rifled through, thinking back over what I'd heard. It made me wonder what had *really* happened to those kids. Mrs. Waterman had said that the authorities were claiming it was a mountain lion or perhaps a black bear. But both animals were rare in this part of Missouri, and an attack on a human was practically unheard of.

The bells over the shop door jingled, jolting me out of my thoughts. I turned around and saw a familiar face. "Hey, Eddie!" I waved.

Eddie O'Connell was a junior in high school. These days, the blonde teenager was considered a 'hottie' by the local girls. But as for me, he'd always be the kid I used to babysit.

"Ivy." He lifted a hand in greeting. "I was wondering if I could talk to you."

"Sure." I gestured to one of the chairs in front of the bookshelves. "Step into my office."

"Thanks." He checked over his shoulder. "Are we alone?" he asked nervously.

His behavior made me reconsider him. Eddie was the youngest brother of our family friend, Violet O'Connell. A year ago, when I'd been working with his sister, Eddie had a bit of a crush on me. So while I was happy to see him, I sincerely hoped he wasn't here to ask me out. However, as I studied him, my stomach dropped.

Something was wrong.

"What's the matter, Eddie?" I asked as I walked over to join him.

"Listen, I wasn't sure who else I could ask about this."

"What's up?" Intrigued, I sat across from him.

"I know a couple of years ago you dealt with that evil spirit on campus. Violet told me about it."

"Yes, the ghosts haunting Crowly Hall." I nodded.

He was trying to psych himself up to talk to me. There was a very real anxiety rolling off him. Now, while I didn't consider myself an empath like my sister Holly, I could almost taste the fear that Eddie was battling. Finally he spoke. "I guess you heard about my friend, Hunter Roland, who was attacked in the woods on Saturday."

"Yes. Mrs. Waterman was in a bit ago and she told me about it. They think it was an animal attack?"

"The park rangers are trying to tell us that it was a bear that got him. But I was there." He blew out a long breath, trying to compose himself. "Ivy, trust me. It *wasn't* a bear. I saw it."

"You were one of the boys in the woods?" I reached out to him and put a comforting hand on his shoulder. "Eddie, what did you see?"

"Well, it had a long tail, was *huge*, had dark shaggy fur, and most importantly..." Eddie reached under his shirt and withdrew a silver-toned pentagram. "I think it was afraid of my amulet."

"Why do you think that?" I asked, studying the pendant.

"Because my pentagram lit up when I got close to it. I hit the thing with a big branch from the fire and that got its attention. But when my pentagram swung free, it glowed. Really brightly. I've never seen my pendant do that before, and I think *that* is what made the monster let go of Hunter."

"I see," I said. My mind was racing as I sat back in my chair. *I'd once seen my own pentagram react in a similar way a few years ago.*

"I didn't know who else to go to. Nobody believes me," Eddie said. "But this isn't a joke! Hunter's leg was mangled!"

"Was it broken?"

Eddie nodded and tucked his amulet away. "In a couple places. He had to have surgery to put it back together."

"What did your folks say about all of this?"

"My family is so mad about what happened." Eddie passed a hand through his hair. "They think I'm making all this up to try and get out of trouble for swiping my dad's beer from the garage."

"Were you drunk that night?" I asked softly.

"No I wasn't! None of us were." Eddie shot to his feet and started to leave. "I thought *you* at least would believe me."

"Before you stomp off," I said, holding up a hand, "I never said that I didn't believe you."

Eddie paused and glanced back over his shoulder.

"Eddie." I sighed. "I know what it's like to have folks roll their eyes and assume you're being dramatic or just making things up."

"Okay," he said, sounding suspicious.

He looked so young standing there, his shoulders hunched defensively in his letterman's jacket, I thought. "Why don't you sit down, and tell me everything that happened that night. In detail."

Eddie took a seat again and told me about their camping trip, and the details of what had happened to his friends. The more he spoke, the more intrigued I became. After we talked he announced he had to get back home. We exchanged phone numbers, I walked him to the door, promised to be in touch, and told him it would be okay.

Flashing a confident smile, I waved goodbye to Eddie. It was hardly a coincidence that Mrs. Waterman had mentioned the creature in the woods moments before Eddie had arrived. "No such thing as coincidence," I murmured, recalling what my mom had always said.

I grabbed a notepad and started to write everything down. Everything I could recall from my conversation with Sharon Waterman, and with Eddie. I covered three pages with notes in what seemed like no time at all.

If what Mrs. Waterman said was true, then Eddie and his friends *weren't* the first ones to come across a monster in the woods. I flipped a page and studied the notes from my conversation with Mrs. Waterman.

I circled the words *the creature was not of this world.* I underlined the words, *Not since '79.* "Which means," I said, as I thought it over. "There's probably a newspaper article about her father's experience. Or perhaps a copy of the picture she spoke about, somewhere."

Mrs. Waterman had described her father's experience as a 'narrow escape', and after hearing about the seriousness of Hunter's injuries, I was inclined to believe her.

Now, all I had to do was start digging. Rubbing my hands together, I headed to the store's computer and booted it up.

This was what I'd been waiting for. A mystery to solve, and a paranormal adventure to sink my teeth into.

This, I decided, was exactly what I needed.

***

I used the rest of my shift to research any other sightings of the creature, and Mr. Waterman's sighting back in December of 1979. To my surprise there were a few random articles and even an outdated website devoted to the Missouri legend of Bigfoot, affectionately known as Momo the Monster.

That website did have a picture they claimed to be taken by Steven Waterman in the winter of 1979. It was grainy, black and white and poor quality. Which made me think it was a digital picture someone had taken of an old newspaper article.

Accompanying the old picture was also a photo of a partial clipping from the William's Ford Gazette. I couldn't see the entire article, but it did mention that several local men had gone into the woods to try and search for the creature. I poked around the website for a bit longer and was disappointed to see that there were no more photos. The website was filled with a collection of anecdotes and personal stories about Missouri's version of Bigfoot from all over the state. However, William's Ford's 'creature' was no more than a footnote.

I checked the Missouri Department of Conservation website about mountain lions or bears and printed a few pages out. I also searched the online catalogue of the local public library, but didn't see any materials that might cross into the local legend. I'd probably have better luck searching the University library. My brother Bran was the University library manager. He had an extensive section on local history and legend. It was one of the things he was most proud of. I made myself a note to talk to Bran about that when I returned home. I emailed myself several more articles from the internet and called it a day.

After I closed the shop at six, I walked down Main Street and took in the holiday lights. I stopped at *The Old World Pub*, grabbed a spot at the bar and ordered a burger and a soft drink. Unsurprisingly, the locals were all talking about the animal attack. I chatted with Miriam the bartender and shamelessly eavesdropped on a couple of older gentlemen who were debating the animal attack with a great amount of enthusiasm. Sadly, I didn't learn anything new.

I headed for home. As I walked up the front steps of the manor house I had to smile at the multicolored lights decorating the front porch. Even thought there was a private entrance to my attic apartment—an outdoor, fancy metal spiral staircase—I rarely used it. Instead I opened the front door of the manor, and discovered pandemonium.

The family had begun to decorate for Yuletide. The long garland of silk holly, ivy, and mistletoe was wrapped around the bannister of the main staircase. It was lit, and the white lights sparkled. The family was currently in the process of setting up the massive eight-foot holiday tree in the foyer. Traditionally, it was tucked behind the curve of the bottom newel stair post, and I'd managed to arrive as they were finishing the assembly.

Morgan, my red-haired three and a half-year-old nephew, was holding on to the bottom of a step ladder. My brother Bran was on said ladder, adding the top section to the artificial tree. My sister-in-law, Lexie, was trying to keep the base of the tree in place.

"Be careful, Bran," she said, and then told her son Morgan to *not* try and climb up the ladder.

Holly, my fraternal twin, was standing on the steps of the manor staircase, holding the middle section of the tree still and attempting to help Bran get the top section of the tree secured.

They were noisy. All talking and laughing at the same time, and I loved them all so much.

My niece, Belinda, toddled unsteadily across the foyer. Her blonde hair was in two tiny pigtails, she was wearing red footie pajamas, and dragging a long piece of silvery garland behind her.

"Hey, baby." I knelt and held out my arms to her.

Belinda's blue eyes lit up when she saw me. "Twee!" she said, rushing forward.

I stood with her in my arms. "Are you helping?" I asked her.

"Uh huh," she said solemnly.

"Hi, Ivy." Bran waved from the top of the ladder.

"I got it!" Holly said triumphantly as she

connected the lights from the middle section to the top of the pre-lit tree.

"Okay, Morgan John," Lexie said. "Now, you can throw the switch and see if the tree lights up."

Morgan scrambled off the bottom step of the ladder, dove under the tree, and hit the button on the light strip. The tree lit up.

"Wights!" Belinda cried, clapping her hands.

All of my niece's L's sounded like W's these days. It was adorable. I pressed a kiss to her cheek. "Yes, the lights are on."

Lexie smiled over at her daughter. "What do you think, baby?"

"Wights, Mama!" Belinda wriggled to get down.

I set Belinda on her feet and she made a beeline for the tree. She'd been only six months old last year at Yuletide. Belinda was going to be a blast this year at the holidays.

"Let's get this tree all fluffed up." Holly said, straightening a few artificial branches.

I hung my coat on the hooks by the front door, pushed up my sleeves, and went over to help.

"We'll decorate it tomorrow night," Lexie said as we worked our way around the tree. "But we thought tonight at least, we could assemble the tree and get it in place."

"Sounds like a plan." I nodded.

Bran stayed on the ladder, adjusting the top section of the tree. His cell phone rang and he pulled it from his back pocket, checked the screen, and scowled. "Damn it."

"Ignore it," Lexie suggested.

"Problem?" I asked.

"The University is trying to hire a replacement for Dr. Meyers," Bran said, putting his phone away, "and everyone is in an uproar."

"Why?" I asked.

"Because folks keep debating on whether or not to give the position of archive director to Autumn or to hire someone new," Lexie said, rolling her eyes. "While several members want to offer the job to Autumn, several others have balked, because she's pregnant."

"Can they actually get away with that?" Holly asked before I could. "Wouldn't that be discrimination?"

"Unfortunately, there are a few older board

members that have very outdated ways of thinking." Bran rolled his eyes. "I've had my fill of their politics."

"Politics in academia?" I pressed a hand to my throat, feigning shock. "Say it ain't so!"

"They'll have to reach a decision after the first of the year," Bran said.

I nodded and listened to the rest of the discussion with half an ear. My mind was busy, thinking about the attack in the woods.

"Ivy." Morgan tugged on my shirt.

I jolted. "Yeah?"

Morgan stared up at me solemnly. "He's coming pretty soon."

I passed my hand over his curls. "That's right. Santa's coming pretty soon."

"No." Morgan frowned. "Not Santa—"

Whatever else he might have said was cut off as Belinda had decided to climb completely under the tree.

"Oh no you don't!" Lexie laughed.

While Belinda began to squeal, Lexie snagged her daughter by the ankles and pulled her out. Once Belinda was back on her feet she took off and began to run in circles around the foyer, laughing. Morgan joined in and the noise was deafening.

Holly came over and slung an arm around my shoulders. "Just another quiet and calm Yuletide with the Bishops."

I slanted my eyes over at my twin. "Well, at least we're never boring."

CHAPTER TWO

A short time later, the little ones were bundled off to bed. Lexie and Bran went to cuddle in the family room. Holly went out, and I trudged up the stairs with the family cat Merlin as company and let myself in my third-floor apartment.

I hit the lights and took a moment to simply enjoy my own personal space. The new walls were painted in a warm white. The slanting ceiling of the attic had been preserved, and its original tongue and groove paneling had a wonderful patina of age. The attic floor was still in great shape. All that had been required was a bit of a polish, and careful furniture placement, to make the area seem as large as possible.

I shut the door and set my purse on the

countertop. My kitchenette was arranged along the right. The white cabinets worked around the brick chimney flue and allowed me a microwave, mini fridge, and a short span of counter with a small sink. A distressed vintage door beyond the kitchenette led to the bathroom and my long, narrow closet.

I adored the bath's slanting walls, vintage looking penny floor tiles and pedestal sink. The custom glass shower surround had been a splurge, but I'd recouped the cost by doing the white subway tile on the shower walls myself—albeit with some help from Duncan. It was good to have a contractor in the family.

In the main living area, I'd arranged my charcoal colored couch along the central left side of the attic walls. A patterned rug anchored it as a living room. My queen size bed was tucked up under the far eaves, with enough room for a nightstand. Finally, opposite of the bed, under the round stained glass window, I'd managed to make a small office area.

It was a cozy space, done mostly in white with pops of black and gray, and it was all mine.

I headed over to my desk, pausing long enough to turn on my lamp on a side table next to my couch. Merlin hopped up on my couch and plopped himself down with a contented chirp.

"Make yourself at home, Merlin." I gave his kitty ears a scratch and went to boot up my laptop. I settled in at my desk under the stained glass window and started printing up everything I'd found online about the "Monster" from 1979.

Pulling a neon marker out from my desk drawer, I went through the pages and started to highlight certain passages. A knock on my door startled me from my research. "Come in!" I called.

My cousin, Autumn Bishop-Quinn, walked in wearing jeans and a bright blue winter sweater. The fabric was pulled tight across her midsection, and I was relieved to notice that her cheeks were nicely pink, and her eyes were bright.

"Hey, Mum!" I grinned at her as she walked over. "You look better."

Autumn brushed her bangs away from her

glasses. "Finally the morning sickness is easing up."

Setting my research aside, I stood up from my desk and walked over to give her tummy a friendly pat. "How are the babies today?"

"Good." Autumn grinned. "We'll hit the fourteen weeks mark in two days."

"Out all on your own?" I raised an eyebrow, making my cousin chuckle. "And walking over from next door and then up the stairs, *unaided*?"

"Pretty daring, eh?" Autumn quipped and took a seat on my couch.

I joined her. "How did you ever escape your squad of protectors?" I said, tucking my tongue in my cheek. Her new husband, Duncan, was understandably protective of my cousin. She'd had a rough time with morning sickness. When they'd discovered they were having twins, both his family and ours had tried to help them out however we could.

"I told Duncan to calm down. Jeez, I can't do a damn thing without somebody jumping in and offering to do it for me," Autumn groused.

"Well, honey you had a tough couple of

months," I said. "We were all worried about you."

Autumn nodded. "And I appreciate everyone's help. More than I can say. But the doctor says we're all doing great, and I wanted to get out of the house for a while. Even if it's only next door. Plus, I'd like to have a conversation that didn't revolve around my being pregnant with twins, before I lose my mind."

"Have you started decorating for Yuletide?" I asked.

Autumn rested her feet on my old coffee table. "This weekend, probably."

"I was thinking of getting a four-foot tree for my apartment, but I want a live one. I love the smell."

Autumn nodded, and her gaze landed on my desk and the papers I had stacked up on it. "What were you working on?"

"Oh, nothing," I tried to sound casual.

Autumn frowned. "Don't bullshit me, Ivy. What are you up to?"

I tucked a lock of hair behind my ear. "I'm doing research on a local legend."

Autumn tilted her head. "Oh yeah?"

"Did you hear about the kids that were attacked over the weekend while they were camping?"

Autumn's eyebrows went way up. "I did. An animal attack or something?"

"Or *something*," I said, filling her in on what Mrs. Waterman and Eddie had told me.

"Did they close the campground and park?" Autumn asked.

"Not that I'm aware of." I wrinkled my nose. "I don't think the park rangers took the boys seriously, either that, or it's all been hushed up."

"There's that midwinter Renaissance Faire in a couple weeks." Autumn narrowed her eyes. "I bet they didn't want to lose the money they would have made from the festival."

"It concerns me," I admitted. "More people tramping through the park and woods means there's more chance of accidental contact with whatever it is that's out there."

"You know," Autumn said, "there was a time I'd have made some snarky comment about you possibly overreacting. But I trust your instincts, and this *is* William's Ford."

"Where magick and weirdness seems to happen on every day that ends with the letter Y." I wiggled my eyebrows at her.

Autumn rubbed her hands together. "This could be the perfect project for you."

I laughed. "That was my reaction too."

"I could go through the local history archives at the museum," Autumn offered. "See if I can find any other mentions of strange animal attacks, or legends of a creature in the local woods before Mr. Waterman's encounter. What year did you say it was, again?"

"It was in 1979."

Autumn nodded and pulled her phone out of her pocket. "Let me make a note so I don't forget." Once she finished she smiled over at me. "I'll do some digging for you."

"That'd be great." I slung my arm around her shoulder. "But I don't want to put you to too much trouble."

"You're not," Autumn said. "I'm an archivist. If there's anything to find, I'll find it. Trust me."

***

The next day I headed to the University library, with the hopes of getting some help from Bran on my research. It wasn't likely I'd stumble across a book on local monsters, but hey, a girl can hope.

My morning spent at the University library was pretty much a bust, even with Bran's help. However, it was totally worth it to see the look on Bran's face when I asked him if he had any books on cryptozoology. Still, my brother was intrigued by the news of the supposed "animal attack". He promised that he'd do some researching on his own and see if there were any reports over the years of bear sightings or even big cats.

I wasn't even sure what exactly to call the animal that had attacked the boys in the woods. Was it safe to say that it was a beast, a creature; or should I simply call it a monster and be done with it? I rolled my eyes at myself. As a Witch researching a possible monster in the woods, it was kind of funny that I sat there sweating over what the most politically correct term would be for it.

For now I liked the term *cryptid.* Since the word was a noun and technically used to describe an unknown animal, or the subject of indigenous legends. I stacked up my reference books and returned them to Bran.

I sent a quick text to Eddie as I left the library, and asked how soon I could meet with his friends Caleb and Rylan so I could obtain more, or even a different perspective from two other people who'd had an up-close and personal with the cryptid.

Eddie texted back that they were all at the coffeehouse and could speak to me now. So I hopped in my old car, drove across town and pulled into a parking spot a block down from the *Black Cat Coffeehouse*.

The three teens were sitting at a four-top table, waiting for me. Eddie O'Connell was the tallest and leanest of the trio. His wavy blonde hair fell over his forehead in a way I bet drove the girls crazy at his school. One of the boys studied me with very large eyes. He was pale, but I wasn't sure if that was because of his auburn hair and fair complexion, or if it was from anxiety. The last of the trio lounged lazily in his chair. The third teen was dark, stockier, and built like a football player—with very broad shoulders and big arms.

Eddie, sweetie that he was, had already ordered a hot chocolate for me. I took a seat at the table and smiled at the trio.

"Ivy," Eddie said, introducing his friends, "this is Caleb Blackthorn and Rylan Hilliard."

"Hey guys." I smiled and sampled the hot chocolate. It was covered in whipped cream with crushed candy cane sprinkled on top. I took another sip, smiled, and got a pad of paper and pen out of my bag.

Rylan went first, and I scribbled notes as he spoke. "That thing was *big*," Rylan said.

"Upright or on all fours?" I asked.

"All fours," Rylan said with a nervous glance around the shop. "I know the police told us it was a bear, but I'm telling you it wasn't. Its fur was too long, and it—whatever it was—smelled horrible."

I made a note about the odor. According to the web research I'd done, the old stories of the Missouri version of Bigfoot, 'Momo', most of the witnesses claimed that the *smell* was the first thing people noticed, even before they saw it. "What color was its fur?" I asked Rylan.

"Dark," Rylan said and thought about it for a moment. "Black, maybe brown."

"It was night when it attacked," Caleb said softly. "It was difficult to see clearly and it all happened so damn fast."

I sipped at the cocoa, listened to Caleb speak, and took more notes. "What texture was the fur?" I asked when he finished.

"Rough, wiry." Caleb answered.

I nodded and wrote down his answer. "Was the fur long or short?"

"Long." Caleb said. "And whatever it was, it stank."

"This is crazy." Rylan suddenly stood, causing his chair to squeak loudly as scooted back. "No one will ever believe us."

At the sound and movement, many of the customers in the coffeehouse stopped talking and began to stare.

Rylan went bright red. "Look, man, I have to go."

"Ry—" Eddie began.

"No." Rylan shook his head. "I told you I would speak to your friend, Eddie, but now that I have—that's it. Talk to that farmer that helped us, or something. Because I don't want to talk about that night ever again."

"What farmer?" I asked.

"Rylan," Caleb said. "Pretending like it never happened ain't gonna help you sleep at night, bro."

Rylan turned his face away and walked straight out the door.

"What's this about a farmer that helped you guys out the night of the attack?" I asked. "Who was he? Did *he* see anything?"

Caleb blew out a breath in frustration. "Dude's name was, McBriar."

"Erik McBriar," Eddie chimed in.

Of course it had to be him, I thought. "What was he doing in the area?" I made sure my voice was casual, and didn't betray my dislike of the man.

"Well..." Eddie appeared a bit bashful. "The park runs along side his property. He told us that one of his farm dogs had been attacked and he'd been out scouting, looking for the tracks of whatever animal had done it."

Even as I dutifully wrote that down, I had to ask. "He was looking for tracks in the dark?"

"I suppose he was scouting around." Eddie leaned forward. "But when he heard us all yelling and Hunter screaming, he came to try and help."

"We were lucky he was there." Caleb said. "Everyone likes to think they'd know what to do in an emergency, but that McBriar guy, *did*."

Despite myself I was curious. "What did he do?"

"He helped us get Hunter out of there, and that probably helped Hunter keep his leg." Caleb swallowed, hard.

I automatically rested my hand on his arm. "That's okay. You don't have to say any more. I get the picture."

"This has been really hard," Eddie said. "But it's nothing compared to what Hunter is going through."

"Damn straight." Caleb crossed his arms across his chest. "Hunter's folks are pretty stressed out too."

Eddie sighed. "Yeah, my mom told me that

they're worried about the hospital bills and the physical therapy he's going to need." He looked down at the tabletop. "It's gonna cost a fortune."

"At least he didn't lose his leg," Caleb said.

I sat back. "I didn't realize that was a possibility."

"Yeah," Eddie said. "The doctors said he was lucky."

"Hey," Caleb said, "did you hear that someone started a fundraiser for Hunter's medical costs?"

"No shit?" Eddie perked up.

"Yeah." Caleb nodded. "Some anonymous donor dropped ten thousand dollars in the fund to get the ball rolling."

"Wow," I said, "well that's some good news, at least."

"It's the best news we've had since Saturday, anyway," Caleb said, sitting back and folding his massive arms.

I tilted my head as my intuition focused on Caleb. "Offensive tackle, right?" I pointed a finger at him.

Caleb blinked. "How'd you know?"

I smiled. “How many colleges are interested in you?”

Caleb’s brows rose in surprise. “A few.”

“I hope you like stripes,” I said, mildly.

“Stripes?” Caleb asked with a small laugh.

“Tiger stripes.”

Eddie elbowed Caleb. “She means, as in Mizzou.”

“You think I’ll end up playing for Mizzou?” Caleb asked me.

“Call it a hunch,” I said.

“That’s where I was considering. But I haven’t told *anyone*.” He rubbed his hand over his chin. “Eddie was right about you.”

“So, Caleb.” I considered his size and strength. “When you dove after Hunter that night, you said that you couldn’t stop Hunter from being pulled away? The cryptid was strong enough to drag all three of you?”

“It yanked us across the ground way too fast,” Caleb said. “I’ve come up against big and strong on the football field, but this...this was something else.”

“Something not of this world?” I asked him, using the same phrase Sharon Waterman had.

"Maybe." Caleb glanced at Eddie. "Look, I get that you and O'Connell are into this magick stuff."

I nodded. "That's one way of putting it."

"All I'm saying is, that I know O'Connell did some kind of spell that night."

"Are you're uncomfortable with that?" I asked, trying to keep my expression neutral.

"Hell, no," Caleb shot back. "Whatever he did probably saved our lives. He ran forward screaming and waving that branch from the fire —"

"Which didn't do a hell of a lot of good," Eddie blurted out.

Caleb acted as if he hadn't been interrupted. "And when he got close, that pentagram he always wears, it lit up. It was so bright that it blinded me."

I nudged Eddie under the table with the toe of my boot. "You were *both* really brave that night."

Eddie met my eyes. "What do we do now, Ivy?" He wanted to know.

"I need to see the campsite and the area of the attack," I said.

"The police have already been there," Caleb pointed out.

I smiled. "But they won't look at it the way I will."

"Like a Witch would?" Caleb guessed.

Eddie nodded. "Exactly. Maybe we could find something out there that everyone else missed."

"Well I'm not going to let you two go out there alone," Caleb grumbled.

I batted my eyes at the football player. "You won't *let* me?"

"Not by yourself!" he argued.

"I won't be alone." I smiled. "I'll have you two with me."

"Isn't that big midwinter Renaissance Faire set to be held at the park this month?" Eddie wondered. "I mean, would we even be alone if we went now?"

"They won't start setting up for another week." I checked my watch. "Besides, if we go now, there shouldn't be much traffic."

Eddie sprang to his feet. "Let's go!"

Caleb shoved away from the table. "I can't believe I'm doing this." He stalked to the door and held it open for me. "I'll drive."

"That's great," I said. "I'll need to make a quick stop at my car to pick up my camera and a few witchy supplies first."

***

The campsite in the state park was fairly unremarkable. Caleb parked on the main road and the three of us stood beside it, surveying the site. I adjusted the camera strap around my neck, and when Caleb made a move as if he would walk over, I stopped him by snagging the sleeve of his coat.

"Hold it."

Caleb looked over his shoulder. "What?"

"We need to be loaded up before we barge right in." I reached in the pockets of my coat to pass him a protective pendant and a tumbled stone.

"What's this?" Caleb turned the stone I'd given him over in his hand.

"It's a black tourmaline crystal, with a protection rune *Algiz* painted on it." I explained. "The pentagram is a protective symbol. Put it on."

"Will they actually help?" he asked.

"It sure as hell won't hurt," Eddie said.

After a moment Caleb shrugged. "Here's hoping." He looped the pentagram over his head. Next, he put the tourmaline in his pocket, and waited.

I pulled my own pentagram pendant out from under my coat so it was in full view, and I saw Eddie do the same.

Eddie dipped his hand in his jacket pocket. "I've been carrying these since the attack." He showed me a small clam shell with a natural hole worn through it. The shell had *Algiz* painted on it. He also had a hag stone and a piece of polished labradorite.

"Smart." I nodded to Eddie. "Listen guys," I said. "I want you to stay quiet and let me scan the area first, I want to see what I can pick up on without any direction from you."

"We should stay together, and stay alert," Caleb said.

I smiled. "Of course." Together the three of us walked to the site. It had been dry since the night of the attack and it was easy to see where their tent had been pitched. There were still a few half-burnt logs in the fire pit, and as I walked slowly around the fire, I paused and framed in a few shots. I took several pictures of the campsite and the surrounding woods.

As I circled the fire pit, my stomach dropped. The hair on the back of my neck rose and my intuition was suddenly screaming at me. *Here,* I realized. *Hunter was struck right here.* “This is where Hunter went down,” I said.

“That’s right.” Eddie nodded, looking a bit pale.

“And he was dragged off in this direction,” I said, pointing toward the woods.

“Yes,” Caleb said. “Rylan and I jumped after Hunter, but it pulled us all with him.”

I could almost hear the echoes of Rylan’s screams. Eddie stepped beside me and I reached for his hand.

Without warning, the present fell away from me and suddenly I was watching the scene as it happened. It was like I was there with them.

The four boys were sitting and laughing around the campfire, when a loud snap in the dark woods behind them had them falling to silence.

"What the fuck?" Hunter flinched as the sounds of something moving through the brush drew closer.

Eddie's head snapped around to survey the area. "Quiet!" he hissed the warning.

The three other boys turned as one and peered into the dark woods surrounding them, but their night vision was shot thanks to staring into the flames of the campfire.

Caleb stood up. "Who's out there?"

There was silence for a moment and then a low rumbling growl came from the darkness of the woods.

"Oh my god." Rylan fumbled with his flashlight, clicked it on, and aimed it toward the woods.

"Do you suppose it's a deer?" Hunter whispered.

"Deer don't growl, dumb-ass," Caleb hissed, snatching the flashlight away from Rylan to shine it into the woods himself.

Together, the boys stood, waiting. And as one they jumped when something began to move through the woods toward them.

"Maybe it's a park ranger," Rylan's voice shook slightly, even as he reached for his pocketknife.

"No," Eddie said quietly. "It feels wrong." He cast his magick out and into the dark woods, trying to get a feel for whatever was out there. "Earth, air, water and fire," he whispered, "illuminate and make the flames go higher." With a subtle gesture, his magick had the campfire billowing up with a whoosh.

The rising flames briefly illuminated the little campsite. But there was nothing he could see, except their tent and the truck parked behind it.

Eddie pulled his pentagram pendant out from under his sweatshirt. The instant his fingertips touched the metal of the amulet, his senses were magnified. "There's something watching us from the cover of the woods. We need to get out of here," Eddie told his friends.

And then all hell broke loose.

Hunter went down. He was standing upright by the fire one second—and the next, he was on the ground, screaming as something dragged him away from the other boys.

"My leg! My leg!" Hunter cried.

"Hunter!" Caleb yelled and dove after him, and then he too was being dragged away. Rylan dove after Caleb, and Eddie grabbed one end of a long branch from the campfire and jumped after them.

The next few moments were horrible. Hunter continued to scream in terror as Caleb and Rylan tried to keep Hunter from being pulled into the woods. But it didn't work. All three of the boys ended up skidding impossibly fast along the ground.

With a primal scream, Eddie ran after them, waving the flaming piece of wood. As soon as he got close, he swung the branch like a baseball bat and connected solidly—with something.

Whatever it was it seemed to recoil from the now illuminated metal pentagram that hung around Eddie's neck.

The light from the pendant was almost blinding, but Eddie took another swing, and this time he met air. "Shit!" He staggered from missing his target. The creature had released its grip on Hunter—and that had bought them all a few precious seconds.

There was a horrible roar, followed by crashing sounds as whatever had attacked them fled back to the darkness and cover of the woods. Eddie's pentagram abruptly dimmed, and lay quietly against his chest. He reached down and hauled Rylan to his feet. Caleb climbed to his feet too, and together the boys half dragged—half carried Hunter across the little clearing and towards the truck.

I shuddered as the vision left me. I let go of Eddie and sat my ass directly on the ground, before I fell over.

"Ivy!" Eddie's voice was sharp. "Hey, are you okay?"

I shook my head hard, in the hopes that the vision of the past would completely leave me. "I read your memories."

"I didn't know you could do that!" Eddie hunkered down in front of me.

"Neither did I." I blew out a breath. "I *saw* what happened that night. Holy shit, you guys! You were so lucky to have gotten out of there."

Caleb tipped his head over to one side. "You gonna be okay?"

"Yup. Give me a second." I pulled up some

stabilizing energy from the ground for another moment and then climbed to my feet.

Eddie helped me stand and I surveyed the campsite with new eyes.

"Ivy?" Eddie asked, nervously.

"Come on." I motioned for the boys to follow me, and following my instincts, I began to walk slowly in the direction that the boys had been pulled that night. I went about twenty feet, stepped into the woods proper, and suddenly felt as if I'd hit an energetic brick wall. "What the hell?" I stopped, looking carefully around. "There's a block here," I said. "Some sort of magickal barrier."

"This is where it let go of Hunter." Eddie explained.

That felt right to me. I looked around again, wondering what I was missing. "Is this where your pentagram lit up, Eddie?" I checked mine, it lay quietly against my coat, and the boys' pendants weren't reacting either.

Turning in a slow circle, I searched for the cause of the barrier. My solar plexus was painfully tight, so I *knew* I was close. But the harder I looked, the less I saw that would explain the phenomenon. There was nothing noticeable that might have created a natural magickal barrier, no stream, or hawthorn trees. Just maple, sycamore and a few oak trees.

The wind shifted, blowing strongly from the north causing the last of the leaves to fall to the ground. I tipped my head back and spotted something low in the sycamore branches. Something unusual.

"Well, hello there," I said.

"*What*?" Caleb's voice rose in concern.

CHAPTER THREE

I pointed over our heads. “Eddie, do you see that?”

“*Phoradendron leucarpum*,” Eddie breathed the words.

“Say what?” Caleb scowled at Eddie.

“Mistletoe,” I clarified for him.

“You mean like the Christmas mistletoe that people kiss under?” Caleb asked.

“More like the magickal mistletoe that was prized by the ancient Druids and other Pagans,” I clarified.

“No shit?” Caleb said.

“No shit,” I said. “Legend has it that the Druids gathered it with golden sickles for their rituals and celebrations.”

Eddie walked to stand directly underneath

the mass of green vegetation. "Did you guys know that it's actually the European mistletoe, *Viscum album,* that is typically sold for the holidays?"

"Right." I nodded. "But that particular variety of mistletoe doesn't grow in Missouri."

Caleb frowned up at the plant. "So what the hell is that?"

"The herb overhead is correctly identified as *Phoradendron leucarpum*," I explained. "Otherwise known as American mistletoe."

"Okay," Caleb said. "And this is significant because?"

"Because it's rare to find it growing this far north in Missouri." I framed in the mass of foliage and took several pictures. "Sometimes called 'witches' brooms', the American mistletoe, is a hemiparasitic plant."

"Witches' brooms?" Caleb shook his head. "Parasitic?"

"Mistletoe prefers to grow in trees with softer wood," Eddie said. "Like the sycamore tree. Mistletoe actually feeds off the nutrients in the tree."

Caleb shrugged. "Yeah, and the plant info is

fascinating O'Connell," he said dryly. "But I'm wondering why we didn't see this big old bunch of mistletoe while we were camping."

Eddie squinted up at the plant. "Probably because not enough leaves had fallen from the trees yet."

Caleb tucked his hands in his pockets. "Since this is the spot where the creature let go of Hunter, do you guys think it was scared off by the mistletoe or something?"

"Maybe," I said. "Folklore states that the mistletoe could repel evil spirits and malicious faeries. Which makes me wonder..."

"What are you thinking, Ivy?" Eddie asked.

I held up a hand asking for silence as I stood beneath the mistletoe. The area was still ripe with the vibes of the attack. No wonder I'd been hit with a vision of the event. "I'm betting it was a *combination* of Eddie's magick, the protective amulet he was wearing, and the mistletoe that repelled the cryptid," I finally said.

Eddie thought that over for a moment. "I know that intense emotions make for stronger magick."

I nodded. "Considering that you were fighting for your friend's life, your survival instincts would have punched your magick out harder than ever before."

"Hey," Eddie said to Caleb, tilting his head toward the tree. "I want to get some of that mistletoe. If it helped stop that creature—"

"Cryptid," I corrected.

"Sure, cryptid," Eddie said. "But if that plant helped stop it, then I damn sure want to be carrying some of it for protection."

I smiled. "Good idea."

"Caleb," Eddie said, giving his friend a light punch in the arm. "Boost me up."

Caleb balked. "I'm not hoisting your skinny ass up in the air, O'Connell."

I rolled my eyes as the two of them began razzing each other. "Boys, boys," I said. "If *I* stood on Caleb's shoulders, I could probably reach the lower leaves."

"Do you have any gloves in your coat?" Eddie asked.

"I do." I handed Eddie my camera and pulled out a pair of thin gloves from my coat pocket. "I have wet wipes too."

"Wipes? Gloves?" Caleb asked. Why do you need those? Are there thorns or something?"

"Mistletoe is toxic," I explained.

"We have to warn people about mistletoe at the flower shop every Christmas," Eddie said.

"Seriously?" Caleb gaped at us.

"Its stems, leaves, and berries contain phoratoxin," Eddie said. "And I know that by heart, because I've rattled it off to enough customers over the years. But if mistletoe is ingested, it *can* cause blurred vision, nausea and diarrhea."

"I get the picture." Caleb made a face. "What I want to know is, if that's a magickal plant associated with old Pagan rituals, what's it doing in a Christian holiday?"

"I'll explain how the Pagan celebration of Yuletide was taken over another time, bro," Eddie said.

So with an assist from Eddie, I found myself standing on Caleb's broad shoulders and gathering sprigs of the mistletoe. I pinched the outer stems off and slowly handed them down to Eddie. Once I'd gathered several sprigs, Eddie helped me down.

We wiped off our hands and then I took a few more minutes and got some additional shots of the woods. The leaves were pretty much gone, but it was still beautiful, and almost haunting in a way. "Do we have enough time to go for a hike?" I wondered out loud.

"Are you crazy?" Caleb asked me. "I wouldn't go back in there without a gun."

"Don't have my gun on me," I said calmly. "I'll be sure to have it when I come back."

Caleb's eyes flared wide. "I hope you're joking about that."

"What's the matter Blackthorn? Haven't you ever met a girl who's gone deer and pheasant hunting before?"

"You? You've gone hunting?"

"With my father in Iowa," I told him. "I have a shotgun and a hunting rifle, and my dad bought me a Smith & Wesson .380 handgun a few years ago."

Caleb sputtered.

"Before you make some sexist comment," I warned him, "I'm a very responsible gun owner. I practice at the range with my sister-in-law—she's a police officer—and I *do* have a concealed carry license."

Caleb shut his mouth. "I guess you told me."

Eddie checked his watch. "Sunset will be in an hour. There's no time for a hike you guys, and we shouldn't be here after dark."

"Agreed." I stared longingly at the woods. I really wanted to go explore the nearby hiking trails to see what I could find, but realistically, if the police and park rangers hadn't seen any animal tracks or signs of large predators, I doubted I would find any. However, the pull I felt toward the woods was very real. Visceral in a way.

I'd have to come back again tomorrow and look around on my own. But when I did, I'd be sure to be armed. Sure, I could probably repel a human attacker with my magick, but after hearing about the extent of Hunter's injuries and *seeing* the event...

I didn't want to take any chances.

***

I did my shift working at the family's store the next morning, and managed to put in a quick call to my cousin, Autumn. I brought her up to speed on what the boys and I had found yesterday while poking around at the campsite. She warned me to be careful and said she was still searching through the local history archives. I didn't bother to mention that I was planning on going for a hike. I didn't want her fretting over it—especially in her condition.

I checked the local paper. There was nothing about animals on the McBriar farm being attacked. The incident with the boys wasn't being featured anymore either. I frowned over that. Seemed to me they were shrugging the whole incident off rather quickly. I sent my sister-in-law Lexie a quick text, and asked if the police were doing any more investigating into the attack. She messaged back that the whole incident had been passed over to the conservation department.

During a lull at the shop I called the local park department and asked about the animal attack, and if the public was being warned to stay out of the woods. My questions didn't go over very well. I was put on hold and bounced around to several different people. None of whom would give me a direct answer, they'd only transfer me to someone else. Eventually I hung up, frustrated by it all.

After my shift ended at noon, I zipped home, changed clothes into something more suitable for a hike and "Witched up". I put my most protective amulets on, and also had a sachet bag filled with the mistletoe I'd gathered in my pocket.

Erring on the side of caution, I also clipped my waist holster in place. I drove back to the campsite and parked my car in a public parking area. The temperatures were hovering in the high 40's so it was an ideal day for hiking. However, there were only a few other cars in the lot, which didn't surprise me—folks were still a tad skittish.

I scanned the big map displayed near the trail head. I had half expected some sort of warning to be posted, but there was none. I double-checked and confirmed that the path to the scenic overlook was directly behind the campsite where the boys had had their encounter.

I popped the trunk and reached in to unzip

the gun case. Double checking to ensure that the .380's safety was on, I quickly slipped the gun in the waist holster and pulled my red padded vest over it. Leaving the vest unzipped, I closed the trunk and began to walk toward the camp site.

It was quiet and peaceful. The sun was shining through the bare branches of the trees, and I took my time exploring the woods just past the campsite. I kept an eye out for more mistletoe, didn't see any, and of course I kept my eyes peeled for any movement in the woods from a large animal. I spotted a few deer, they froze in place until I walked past, and slowly went back to foraging. There were squirrels and birds, of course. But other than that, nothing.

I took my time sensing the area as I went, checking to see if anything appeared to be out of place, but everything *felt* normal. After all, if there were deer in the immediate area, then a predator was most likely not.

I found the scenic overlook and stopped to admire the view. Rocks jutted out and the trees were twisted and growing up and between slabs of limestone. The view of the Missouri river was spectacular, and I wished I had my camera with me. Instead I pulled my cell phone out of my back pocket and snapped a few quick photos.

I indulged myself for a few more moments and then tucked my phone away. My senses were telling me that nothing was wrong. Whatever had been in the area the night of the attack was gone. I turned back, retracing my steps and walking back toward the camp site.

I caught the sound of cheerful whistling before I heard the footsteps. Someone else was out taking a walk, and I automatically moved to the side of the path to let them pass. The path angled to the right and as I came around a cluster of trees, what I saw had me doing a double-take.

A man ambled along the path. He was tall, fit, and wearing the most elaborate holiday costume that I had ever seen. His salt and pepper hair flowed to his shoulders, and he also sported a long gray beard.

In seconds I summed up his clothing. He wore over-the-knee boots, some type of leather leggings, an open linen shirt, and it was all topped off by a long, hooded fur trimmed jacket. It was a woodland Santa meets Viking sort of costume.

"Wow, that's some fancy get-up," I said as he approached. "Very Viking Santa. You went all out."

The man stopped a few feet away from me. He appeared to be as shocked to see me as I was at seeing him. "Hi," he said after a moment.

"Hey there." I nodded. "You're about a week early for the midwinter Renaissance Faire."

He pushed back the hood on his jacket and I noticed his eyes were blue. I estimated him to be in his fifties, and the man was lean and athletic. He spoke, but I had no idea what he'd said.

"Jeez!" I smirked. "Was that Danish or something?" *Leave it to me to stumble across a midwinter Renaissance Faire cast member in the woods...At least I hoped he was a cast member,* that last thought had my stomach tightening.

He stood there, silently studying me.

"Tell you what, Viking Santa," I said. "You

might want to stay alert while you're out here giving your costume a test run. There was an animal attack in these woods last week." Since he continued to stare, I decided to get away from him. "Well, buh-bye now." I moved past him and started walking farther along the path.

"Wait," he said, dropping a hand on my shoulder.

I swung around with my own hand over the holster. "Back off," I warned him.

He spotted the holster and held up his hands. "I meant you no harm, Ivy," he said.

Oh, shit. He knew my name. My heart began to speed up and I moved farther back from him to be on the safe side.

I'd never reached for my gun because of a human threat in my life. I also knew better than to take it out of the holster unless I was committed to using it. I left the gun in place, because I honestly couldn't tell if the man was a threat or merely confused. And that put me on edge.

"Who are you?" I asked.

"I have many names."

"Wow, you're not going to break character,

are you?"

He shook his head. "You may call me, *Julemanden.*"

"Yule-a-manden?" I tried to sound it out.

"*Ja.*" He smiled, standing perfectly still, and the look he gave me was damn near paternal.

Almost as if he was disappointed in me.

The weird thing was I didn't detect any sort of malice or threat coming from the man. What I sensed was benevolence. I wasn't sure whether to admire his commitment to the role he was portraying, or if he was just odd.

"Why don't you do us both a favor and move along?" I said.

"You spoke of an animal attack?" His voice had a thick accent. "Is that why you are afraid?"

"Last week there was an attack on a local boy," I said.

"Ah, he was up to no good," he said. "Out with his friends in the woods, yes?"

"Sure." I drew the word out. *He must have caught wind of the local gossip,* I thought.

The man sighed. "At this time of year those boys should know better than to misbehave so badly. The wild hunt was sure to find them."

"Well..." I said, figuring I'd humor him. "I suppose they'll all be on the naughty list."

"*Måske*—maybe," he said, as he appeared to think that over.

"Musky?" I frowned over the strange word.

"I must go." He nodded and continued down the path. "*Farvel.*"

"Huh?" It sounded like he's said *farewell*. Only with a V instead of a W.

"*Glædelig Jul,*" he called from over his shoulder. With a wave, he moved quickly over the dirt path and was soon out of sight.

"Flare-lee yule?" I tried to wrap my tongue around his words.

I waited a couple of moments, trying to settle myself down. I still wasn't sure if I'd overreacted to the man or not. I blew out a long breath and start walking again, making sure to stay extra vigilant for the rest of my hike.

I thought over my encounter with the Renaissance Faire player. He'd never broken character, not even when asked about the attack. Though I couldn't imagine why he'd been hiking in his full costume. Maybe it was simply a clever gimmick designed to drum up business for the Faire. *Local citizens report encountering Viking Santa in the woods. Film at ten,* I thought and chuckled. Oh well, the guy was sure to be a hit with all the children who attended the Faire.

I finally reached the end of the trail and rolled my shoulders, attempting to relax. I walked to my car, casually checking, but didn't see the man anywhere in the parking lot.

"Perhaps he jumped in his sleigh and took off," I said to myself.

After stowing my gear in the trunk, I decided to check and see if the man was still around. I drove my car through the campground loop a couple of times wondering if he was out there poking about, but I didn't see him anywhere. Which surprised me.

I mean, how hard would it be to spot a guy in full costume with long silver hair and a beard?

***

An hour later I had morphed back from Ivy the part-time amateur paranormal investigator —to Ivy the hopefully full-time photographer. I was headed out again, this time to the local tree farm to scout out the best location for the engagement photos that I was scheduled to take the next morning.

I liked the idea for the portraits, it was both romantic and festive. However, I was facing a potential problem with my client's request. The local Christmas tree farm was owned by the McBriar family, and the tree farm was run by Erik McBriar.

Erik McBriar may have come to the aid of Eddie and his friends, but he *hated* my family. He still blamed Holly for the destruction of his sister's antique store. Holly had been an employee of the antique store when Leilah Drake Martin had attacked her a couple of years ago. However, Leilah hadn't been merely satisfied at kicking Holly's ass. She'd also done as much damage to the inventory of the shop as possible, and had stolen some vintage jewelry.

Afterward, Holly had ended up in the hospital, and while she was recovering Erik had approached my sister, encouraging her to quit. He'd told her it was nothing personal. *To each his own,* he'd said. But bottom line? Erik had wanted Holly and magick as far away from his family as possible.

Once word of his treatment of Holly hit town, the older families began boycotting the antique store *and* the new wedding barn venue the McBriars had launched. My cousin, Maggie, had also been set to coordinate a wedding at their rustic venue this past summer. But while touring the farm, she'd had an unpleasant run-in with Erik who'd been publically bashing my family at the time. So Maggie had found a different venue for her clients, and Erik's mouth had ended up costing his family a booking.

But the real kicker had happened a few months ago. Leilah Drake Martin had completely snapped and abducted Maggie's daughter, Willow. She'd held the little girl captive in the McBriar's barn.

Once Maggie had figured out where Leilah was, she and Holly had gone all *Lethal Weapon*, and had driven their car right through the farm's wooden gates to get to the wedding barn. Maggie had faced down Leilah inside, and when all was said and done...Willow was safe, the good Witches had won the day, and Leilah went out on a stretcher, probably never able to walk again.

Once the police and the press had descended on the scene, the publicity from the abduction and Leilah's fall had pretty much put the kibosh on anyone wanting to rent out the old barn for a wedding reception ever again.

Was any of the bad luck surrounding the wedding barn my family's fault? No. But it didn't stop Erik McBriar from hating us all. Which was why I'd had the couple contact his mother, Diane, first. Diane used to run the wedding barn side of the family business. *Used to* being the operative words. Anyway, I'd had a hunch that she would be the most open to the idea.

Even as I packed my camera and lenses, I reminded myself that Diane McBriar was a very nice woman. Everyone in William's Ford knew that the Christmas tree farm was a last-ditch effort to save the McBriar's family business. So, someone doing an engagement photo shoot out at their tree farm was positive PR, and Diane needed all the help she could get.

She'd been delighted at the idea of the couple wanting to take photos there, and to her credit when I'd called to set up appointments to view the property, and then to take the photos, she'd been nothing but gracious.

To that end, I chose my outfit with care. I needed to look professional but still be practical. I laced up my hiking boots over a pair of skinny jeans, layered a black and white plaid flannel shirt over a black tee, and slipped my insulated red vest over that. I double checked my face in the mirror, and was satisfied at the smoky eye and bold red lips. The lipstick was bright, seasonally cheerful, and it matched my vest.

I grabbed my camera bag and purse and headed down the stairs to the second floor to pick up my secret weapon. A weapon guaranteed to be an adorable buffer and to ease my way with the McBriar family at the farm. My nephew, Morgan.

Lexie and Morgan were waiting for me at the second floor landing.

"One test subject, ready for duty," Lexie said.

I grinned at my red-haired nephew who stood in his jeans, boots, and holiday sweater. “Looking good, Morgan.”

“Okay!” He danced in place. “I’m ready to see the Christmas trees!”

“Let’s get going.” I took his coat from Lexie and off we went.

CHAPTER FOUR

I'll say one thing for the McBriar family, they knew how to set a scene. The gravel parking area of their farm stand was about half full, even on a Wednesday afternoon. As I drove slowly in, I spotted a large old wooden shed ahead. It had been converted into a retail area, and its wood exterior had faded to a gorgeous weathered gray. The building was brightened by pine roping, white lights, and above the door a sign was painted announcing it to be the *Mistletoe Mercantile*.

"How cute is that?" I murmured as I parked the car. I couldn't help but smile at the variety of wreaths in several sizes that were displayed on the sides of the building. Each fresh wreath sported white lights, and was trimmed out with a big, bright red bow.

"Look at the Christmas trees!" Morgan shouted

I gazed out over the acres of trees in the distance. Beneath a cloudy gray sky, all the evergreens were planted in neat rows. "Wow," I said. "It's huge. I had no idea."

We climbed out of the car to the sounds of Christmas music playing on a loudspeaker in the parking lot. To the right you could easily see the fields in the distance. To the left, a variety of fresh-cut evergreen trees ranging from three feet to over eight feet in height were stacked upright in wooden racks and awaiting purchase.

Next to the tree racks a classic red Ford pickup was parked. Its tailgate was down and the bed was loaded with a small live tree, a chippy white sign, and a vintage wooden sled. The distressed wooden sign announced, *McBriar's Christmas Tree Farm. Now Open. Cut Your Own.*

I eyeballed that vintage truck and my mind raced with ideas for photos. I pulled my camera bag out, hitched it over my shoulder, and took

Morgan's hand. "Let's go find Diane," I said, and together we walked inside the farm's gift shop.

I pushed open the door to discover a rustic checkout counter. A young family stood checking out with a tree on a cart. A woman wearing a bright red apron was ringing them up, and I took a moment to admire the many fresh wreaths on pegs behind the counter and another vintage wooden sled that was decorated with fresh pine boughs, tartan ribbon, and rusty looking bells.

A smaller live tree was sitting at the end of the checkout area in a big metal tub. It had been decorated with multi-colored lights, dried orange slices, strings of popcorn, cranberries and finally tiny red bows. Beside it, on a big stand someone had written on a chalkboard that photos with Santa would be available on Tuesday and Friday evenings, and all day Saturday and Sunday.

Clever, I thought, and continued to look around.

There were tables of poinsettias, metal buckets of mistletoe, and more big rustic tables filled with evergreen roping and fresh-cut boughs for decorating. Against the walls, a large display was set up. It was filled with vintage and reproduction Christmas signage, ornaments, rustic wooden crates, and milk cans filled with Yuletide greenery.

There were decorated mini trees and swags, candle holders and rings of artificial berries. Twinkling lights were strung from the rafters, Christmas songs were playing in the background, and the rustic farm holiday vibe they'd set up was perfection.

I wanted to photograph absolutely everything.

"It's Santa's workshop," Morgan breathed.

"Ivy?" I turned at the sound of my name and saw a middle-aged woman walking toward me. She was trim, with salt and pepper hair pulled back in a neat, low ponytail. Her blue glasses matched her eyes and made them pop. She smiled and stuck out her hand. "I'm Diane, we spoke on the phone."

I shook her hand. "Hello Mrs. McBriar, it's nice to meet you. The holiday display you set up in here is amazing."

"Thank you." She grinned. "I've been cherry picking my daughter Ginny's antique finds for almost a year to pull this off."

"I'd love to take some photos of it, if you don't mind," I said automatically.

"Twist my arm," she laughed. "Maybe we could use them on our website."

I nodded. "There you go."

Morgan tugged at my hand. "Can I go look at the little trees?" He pointed to a display table of decorated mini trees in old crates and boxes.

"Yes," I said. "But stay where I can see you."

"Okay!" Morgan sang and scurried over.

"Now," Diane said. "I've arranged for you to be taken out to the best spot in the tree field so you can look around and decide where you'd like to set up for tomorrow. It's a gorgeous location and there's even an old apple tree out there that's covered in mistletoe."

"Nice!" I nodded. "Do you gather it to sell at the stand?"

"We sure do." She grinned. "That's how we came up with the name, *Mistletoe Mercantile*."

"I love that." I smiled. "I brought my nephew along today to use him as a test subject." I tipped my head toward him. “That is if I can ever get him out of here.”

But Morgan was happy to go see the trees in the field. Diane used her walkie-talkie to call a ride for us, and I was smiling and looking forward to scouting out the fields for a good location. A gator type of vehicle zipped around to the front of the barn and pulled to a stop in front of us.

A man in jeans, boots, and a heavy work coat climbed out and focused on Morgan and me. I watched as his eyes traveled from my camera case, back to Morgan, and finally to my face. The smile that he’d been wearing, suddenly wilted.

I studied him back as carefully as he had me. He was tall, and annoyingly good-looking with dark blonde hair and a low-scruff beard. Eyes the same sizzling blue as his mother’s blinked in recognition. “Hello, Ivy,” he said.

My heart sank even as I smiled politely up at his handsome, suspicious face. “Hello Erik.”

“You’re the photographer?”

I inclined my head. “I am.” *You bigoted idiot,* I thought.

"I see." He blew out a long breath.

"Do we get to ride in that?" Morgan asked pointing to the gator.

Erik actually smiled at the boy. "You betcha."

Nobody could withstand my nephew's charm, I thought. Which is precisely why I'd brought him along.

"Hooray!" Morgan yelled and ran straight for the cart.

I half expected a snide comment as we set out, but Erik was polite. He cheerfully answered Morgan's questions as he sat between the two of us. Morgan started to belly laugh as we went zipping across the path to the Christmas tree fields.

"What variety of holiday trees do you have?" I asked politely, when Morgan stopped asking questions.

Erik made a quick turn down a new path. "Balsam fir, Scotch pine, blue spruce, white pine, and Douglas fir."

"How much trouble do the white pines give you?" I said. "They aren't always compatible with Missouri clay soils."

Erik gave me a considering look. "They do okay."

Well, so much for making polite conversation, I thought. I slapped a smile on my face and told myself that I could put up with Erik McBriar for a half hour. I had clients depending on me. If the photo shoot went well, I might even be able to do their wedding next year on my own.

We came to a stop a few minutes later and Erik climbed out. I exited from the other side, determined to be a professional.

I checked my surroundings, and saw that Diane had indeed known where the best spot was. The old apple tree she spoke of stood by itself on a small rise. It was gnarly and twisted, and covered in mistletoe. I made a mental note to get over and photograph that tree when I was finished scouting for the engagement photo shoot. The tree was incredible, and it had an ancient and magickal sort of vibe.

Turning to consider the area, I couldn't see anything other than the rows of Christmas trees and a slice of woods off in the distance. I got my camera out of the case, and my heart gave a good hard bounce when I realized that those woods were actually the park where the boys had been attacked.

"I heard from Eddie O'Connell that you helped him and his friends last week," I said to my reluctant chauffeur.

Erik nodded. "Yes, I did."

"Eddie mentioned you'd also..." I shifted my eyes deliberately to Morgan. "Had an unfortunate incident involving one of your canines, here on the farm?"

"One of the older canines." He used the same word and Morgan stayed oblivious.

"I hope it will recover."

Erik frowned. "It didn't."

"I'm so sorry," I said.

"Catch me!" Morgan hollered at Erik and leapt from the gator. Erik grinned and caught my nephew and swung him to the ground.

"Have you seen anything on the farm to indicate a predator?" I asked. "Tracks or scat from a large animal?"

"No," Erik said. "But we've started taking a few precautions." He slid his eyes toward the back of the gator. I followed his gaze and saw, next to a few old apple crates, a camo rifle case stowed in the back of the vehicle.

"Good." I slipped the camera strap over my head. My father had a gun case similar to Erik's. His was also soft-sided, zippered, and he used it for deer hunting in Iowa.

"I'll wait around until you finish with the photos," Erik said. "I'll be right over there." He turned and pointed down another row. "Give a shout if you need anything."

"Thank you," I said. Knowing there was a gun in the gator, and someone else nearby, did make me feel better. Not that I was afraid for myself, but I didn't want to take chances with Morgan's safety. Not after *seeing* for myself the attack on Eddie and his friends.

Erik gave me a nod and walked away in the direction of the lone apple tree—and I simply couldn't resist. The guy didn't have to be likeable to be photogenic. I lifted my camera, framed him in, and took a few pictures of him from behind as he walked among the rows of Christmas trees.

The temperatures were hovering in the 40's and the breeze was light, so I had Morgan unzip his coat. At first I let him wander around a bit. I took photos of the area, checking the screen of my digital to see how it all looked. I readjusted for the cloudy skies and shot some casual photos of Morgan walking between the rows of the evergreens, and more of him standing, surrounded by the lower branches.

Delighted with the candid shots, I tried for a formal pose. I managed to get him to do a few different poses, but after half an hour, Morgan was getting bored. So I offered up a bribe—*if* he'd consent for a few more formal pictures.

"What do I get?" he asked.

"How 'bout french fries?" I said, knowing full well what his reaction would be.

"French fries!" Morgan shouted happily, and I snapped a few more photos capturing his grin.

"I'd pose for french fries too," Erik said from behind me.

In a good mood from the photos I'd gotten, I sent him a smile. "Yeah, well, fastest way to a man's heart."

He laughed and, to my surprise, leaned over my shoulder. "Can I see some of the photos?"

"Sure." I lowered the camera and flipped

through the digital images so he could view the recent ones of Morgan.

"Those are *really* good, Ivy."

The surprise in Erik's voice had me holding back a snippy retort. I settled for a careful, "Thank you." I slipped the lens cap back on. "Morgan," I called. "Put on your coat, buddy. We need to head back."

"Aww!" Morgan's whine was loud and long.

"It'd be a shame to lose out on french fries." I let the threat hang.

Morgan came straight to me, allowing me to zip up his coat, and he climbed in the gator without another word.

I left my camera around my neck and got settled in beside him. "Would you mind driving over to the apple tree?" I asked Erik. "I'd love to get some photos of the mistletoe."

"Sure," he said, and drove toward the gnarly tree. "I have to gather some for Mom anyway. They have almost sold out at the stand."

Erik pulled over to the tree, turned off the ignition and pocketed the keys. Morgan was happy to sit for a few. He slid immediately behind the wheel of the gator and pretended to drive.

"This will only take me a couple minutes," I said to Morgan.

"Okay!" he called and honked the horn of the gator.

I hopped out on my side and walked around the back of the vehicle. "Let me take a few photos before you start harvesting," I said, since Erik was already under the tree.

"Hang on a second." He reached under the tree and picked up a long pruning pole from the ground. "Let me get this out of your way. We leave the pruner out here this time of year." He stepped back, moving out of my shot.

I framed the tree in and took several quick photos. I walked all around and under the tree, snapping as many pictures as I could from various angles. "Okay," I told him, stepping well out of the way. "Go ahead."

"This will only take me a second," he said, and untied a heavy plastic bag from the business end of the pruner. He tucked the bag in his coat pocket and went to fetch the crate from the back of the gator. He stood and considered the tree, looking for the best place to prune.

I framed him in and took a few more photos as he worked. When I realized he was just going to let the mistletoe fall, I let the camera drop to my chest and rushed forward to grab the branches before they hit the ground.

"Got it!" I cried triumphantly.

"What the hell are you doing?" he asked.

"You're never supposed to let mistletoe hit the ground when you gather it."

"Why?"

"It will lose all its magickal properties if it does." I walked over to the apple crate and set the cluster of green leafy twigs gently inside.

He rolled his eyes. "Seriously?"

"Don't go all *bah-humbug* on me, McBriar. Mistletoe is a plant of peace. According to legend it represented reconciliation between enemies."

"My grandmother says kissing beneath the mistletoe is a Scandinavian custom." He reached out with the pruner again. "I'm trying to remember the story she told me about it."

"Balder, the son of Frigga, and Loki the trickster?" I asked. "Does that ring any bells?"

"Sounds familiar." He shrugged. "I'm going

to gather a little more."

I saw where he was reaching and moved to intercept. "I'll catch it."

I snagged the second batch and added that to the crate as well. Erik tied the bag back over the metal end of the pruner and put it back where it had been. I scooped up the crate and carried it to the back of the gator for him.

"I'm driving!" Morgan laughed. "Look, Ivy!"

"You're doing great," I called back.

"You didn't have to carry it." Erik took the crate from my arms and slid it in the back of the gator.

"It's not heavy and I don't mind." I said, doing my best to be courteous and even smile at him. Truth be told, I was sorely tempted to kick him in the shins. Instead of giving into my desire, I pulled a packet of wipes out of my pocket and wiped my hands clean.

He reached out toward me. "You have mistletoe in your hair."

"Oh." I did my best not to flinch back in surprise.

He stepped closer, and plucked out a few

leaves. "Reconciliation between enemies, eh?"

The last thing I'd ever expected was to be practically standing in Erik McBriar's arms. I narrowed one eye at him. "Why ask, if you're only going to make fun of the answer?"

He smiled down in my face and my heart skipped a beat. "I wasn't making fun of you. I was simply curious."

"All right then." I cleared my throat. "Mistletoe is sacred to the Druids, banned by Christianity and *yes*, it is a plant of peace."

He studied the tiny leaves in his hands. "So where did all the stuff about kissing under it originate from?"

"If enemies met under the mistletoe at Yuletide they were supposed to lay down their weapons and exchange a kiss instead of beating the crap out of each other." I raised an eyebrow. "However, I am willing to make an exception in your case, McBriar."

His smile was self-deprecating. "Come on, I'll drive you back to the stand."

"You're such a gentleman," I muttered, and he seemed to find that hilarious.

Morgan slid over, I climbed back in, and Erik

started up the gator. We'd gone about fifty yards when he stopped and let out a loud piercing whistle. "Buck!" he called, and a big yellow lab came running toward us.

The lab jumped in the back of the gator. It was obviously an old routine for them, and the dog promptly stuck his head over the front seat to sniff Morgan's hair.

"Hello, Buck." I patted the dog's head as Morgan giggled.

"We've been trying to keep closer tabs on the farm dogs," Erik said. "Buck is used to having the run of the place, but I want to keep him close."

My heart broke for the dog they'd lost. "I don't blame you."

Erik waited until the dog sat before he started up again. He went even faster this time and had Morgan shouting in delight. "Faster!"

I considered the lab as he sat in the back. "The dog won't fall out, will he?"

"Nah." Erik grinned. "He's used to riding in the gator."

It was hard to hold on to any resentment with Morgan belly-laughing on the ride back to the farm stand. I thanked Erik for the ride, while Morgan climbed out and the dog jumped down.

Diane came out of the store with a smile. “Everything go well?” she asked.

“Perfect,” I said as Morgan dropped to his knees to hug the dog. Behind them, that old vintage truck sat there looking like a holiday commercial. “Say, Diane,” I began, “would you mind if I took a few more photos?”

“Of course you can,” she said.

“I might need a couple of things from the store. As props,” I explained.

“What are you thinking of doing?” Erik asked.

Since he sounded genuinely curious, I answered him. “I want to take some photos of the trees, that old sign, *and* the truck.”

“Knock yourself out,” Erik said.

“Is it all right if I photograph Morgan in the back of the truck with your dog?” I stopped in my consideration of the truck and the best angles to return my attention to the McBriars. “You could probably use it on your website for advertising.”

“I *love* that idea!” Diane said. “Erik and I are

happy to help. What do you need?"

I wondered if Erik was as happy about 'helping' as Diane was, but I didn't want to miss my chance. I had a feeling. This would be important.

It only took a couple of minutes, but I added a big fresh wreath and some pine boughs. Getting Morgan to climb up in there—sans coat and with the dog—was no hardship at all. I stepped back, framed them in, and started taking photos. Making sure to get the old sign in the shot and the freshly cut holiday trees in the background, I took a couple dozen pictures. I was so busy trying to get the perfect composition that I didn't even realize it had been Erik swapping out or changing around props as I asked.

I checked the screen of the camera, flipped through the images, and smiled. "These are going to be great."

On cue, Buck jumped down and Morgan started to fidget. Before I could reach for him Erik swung Morgan down from the bed of the truck. "Here you go, buddy."

"Morgan." I tousled his red curls. "You did

awesome! I'm getting you the biggest french fries they make, a cheeseburger, *and* a chocolate shake."

"Yes!" Morgan jumped up and down.

Diane held out Morgan's coat. "Put your coat back on, sweetie," she said.

Morgan dutifully complied. "I like your dog," he told Diane.

Buck sat in front of Morgan and lifted a paw to shake.

Diane smiled. "I'd say the feeling is mutual." She nodded toward the camera. "Can I see?"

"I want to surprise you," I said. "When I come back in the morning with Shawna and Brian, I'll have some proofs for you to look at then."

"I'm so excited!" Diane laughed. Her name was called, and she started back toward the farm stand. "See you in the morning."

I tucked the camera back in the bag and held out my hand for Morgan. We started for my car, and to my surprise, Erik and his dog followed us. I was further shocked when Erik opened the car door for Morgan. "What time will you be here in the morning?" he asked.

"Eight o'clock," I answered as Morgan climbed in the back seat. "Diane said we should come in before opening so we could have the field to ourselves."

"Okay." Erik nodded.

"Thank you for the help today," I said, reaching for my door handle.

Erik reached past me and opened the car door himself. "I'll look forward to seeing those pictures."

I was so caught off-guard by how courteous he was that it took me a moment to reply. "Yeah, well." I put the camera case on the front seat. "I'll fiddle with them a bit and tweak 'em. But I think your mom will be happy."

Erik nodded. "See you around, Ivy."

"Erik." I nodded and got in the car. I started it up and pulled out of the parking space. I flashed my eyes to the rearview mirror and saw that Erik McBriar was standing hip-shot in the gravel lot and watching me as I drove away.

***

After dinner with Morgan, who devoured his

burger and fries, I happily worked on the tree farm photos of my nephew for the rest of the evening. I also took a call from the editor at the local paper. He asked if I'd be interested in providing photos for an article that they were about to run on shopping small businesses for the holidays. I bit back a laugh, told him that I would be, and then described to him what I was currently working on.

He was curious about my tree farm photos, so while we were on the phone I emailed him a few thumbnails containing the best images of Morgan and the dog in the old red truck. To my delight, he wanted my photos for the article, and the town's tourism website.

I promised to get back to him by tomorrow, once I obtained permission from the McBriars. I already knew Bran and Lexie would be proud to have Morgan featured in the photos, so there was no problem there. After the editor's call, I continued to work, tweaking and polishing the best images, and I was thrilled with the results.

I loaded the best of the pictures onto a flash drive, printed out a release form for the McBriar family to sign, and fell into bed sometime after midnight.

CHAPTER FIVE

My alarm went off disgustingly early, and I staggered toward the mini-fridge to get myself a soda. I popped the top and chugged deeply as I made my way to the bathroom shower. Later, I stood with hair and makeup finished and considered my outfit choice.

Today, I pulled on a pair of dark blue jeans and layered a heavy, plaid shirt over a red turtleneck. It was a variation on a theme from the day before. However, I would be tramping my way across tree fields, hauling cameras, my tripod, and there was mud. So practical and festive was smart. I added the family crest pendant to my outfit and the silver crescent moon lay sparkling against the red sweater. I dropped a white infinity scarf around my neck, zipped up my red insulated vest, and was out the door by 7:30am.

When I arrived at the McBriar Farm, I was surprised to discover that the farm's gift shop was open. Shawna and Brian arrived shortly after I did, and today it was Erik's father, Ezra, who drove the three of us out to the fields in a serviceable four-door pickup.

He dropped us off, said he needed to check on some trees, but that he'd be nearby. He told me to toot the horn on the truck when we were ready to go. He gave us a wave and as he turned to go, I noted that he was wearing a holster at his waist. My intuition told me that Ezra was actually walking about looking for any signs of a large animal, as opposed to 'checking trees'.

Seemed like the McBriars were taking the animal attack seriously. I needed to remember to ask more about the dog they'd lost as soon as I had the chance, too. But I'd ask his parents. It'd be for the best if I avoided the Witch-hating Erik.

For now I shifted my attention back to my clients. Shawna and Brian were standing hand in hand and smiling into each other's eyes. I set my bag on the ground, pulled out my camera, and got down to business.

The couple was a dream to work with. Relaxed and happy, they were eager to start the photo shoot. Shawna had gone with a trendy boho style for her pictures. She had worn a long red skirt, boots, a pretty sweater and plaid scarf. Brian had on a cool gray sweater, a red scarf and jeans. I started out by taking the more formal, posed photos first.

Afterward, I turned them loose to wander around through the rows of the trees. I told the couple to feel free to kiss or cuddle, and I followed them around like a paparazzi, taking candid shots for the remainder of our session.

When the timer on my phone buzzed, our forty-five minutes were at an end. I opened the door of the truck, gave the horn a quick beep, signaling that we were ready to go. "Hey guys," I said to the couple. "I'd like to get a few additional photos of you by that classic Ford truck in front of the gift shop, if you don't mind."

"That'd be great." Shawna smiled.

Ezra arrived and we loaded up. As soon as

we got back to the parking lot I jumped out and got the couple into position by the vintage red truck. I needed to work quickly before the farm opened for the day.

This time the tree farm sign was too distracting for the portrait. I let the camera fall to my chest and was about to climb in the back of the truck to lay it down myself, when Erik appeared.

"What do you need?" he asked, graciously.

I blinked him back into focus. "Can you lay the sign in the truck bed down?"

"Sure." He hopped up in the bed, and in a few moments had the sign out of view.

"Perfect," I said, and as soon as he cleared my shot I started taking photos again. I framed the couple in, shifted my perspective, and snapped away. I stopped, checked the digital screen and smiled. Third from the end was the money shot.

I motioned the couple over to show them and Shawna let out a quiet, "Oh, *wow.*"

Brian pressed a kiss to his fiancée's temple, and I promised to have the proofs ready for them to choose from within a few days.

“We’re opening up,” Ezra called out.

I waved off the happy couple and secured the camera in my bag. I placed my camera case on the front seat of the truck and set to work putting the truck display back to its original look.

I climbed in the truck bed and pulled the tree farm sign back up so that it would be viewable once again as folks drove into the lot. Stepping back to the very edge of the truck bed, I considered the composition, and made a few adjustments to the entire holiday display. “There,” I said. “That looks good.”

Satisfied that it all looked sharp, I hopped down, gathered my things, and went back to my own car to stow the camera and to retrieve my laptop. My mind completely on showing the photos I’d taken yesterday to Diane, I shut the door, turned, and bounced right off Erik McBriar.

“I beg your pardon,” I said.

He steadied me with a hand on my arm. “Careful.”

I resisted the urge to yank away from him. This was the guy who hated my sister and was anti-Witch. I didn't like that he was being so solicitous. It made me wonder what he was up to. "Is your mom handy?" I asked. "I have those proofs from yesterday to show her."

"She's right inside," he said. "Can I help you with anything else?"

I started toward the shop's door and forced a tone of cheer into my voice. "You can remind me to pick out a four-foot tree for my apartment before I leave today. Otherwise, I'll probably forget."

"Sure." Erik seemed taken aback by the request. "I didn't know you celebrated Christmas."

I made sure that I had a neutral expression on my face before I opened my mouth. "We celebrate the winter solstice."

"And you decorate Christmas trees?"

I prayed for patience. "Maybe you aren't aware of the fact that it wasn't until the 1950's that churches even allowed decorated evergreen trees inside the sanctuaries."

His eyebrows went up. "No, I didn't know that."

"Do you know why they didn't?" I asked

gently.

Erik folded his arms over his chest. "No, why?"

"Because they considered a decorated evergreen tree to be too *Pagan*."

"That can't be true."

I pulled a deep breath in through my nose, and met his eyes. "Tell you what Erik, why don't you go to the library and look up the history of where all the popular Christmas traditions actually came from? You'll be amazed at what you discover." I smiled sweetly. "That is, if the thought of finding out the truth doesn't scare you too much."

While he gaped at that, I calmly went inside. To my surprise, Erik followed me and hung around while I booted up my laptop. I told myself to ignore him. My instincts were shouting that this would be an important meeting, and I wouldn't allow Erik McBriar to ruin it. I'd be polite and professional *come hell or high water*—as my cousin Maggie liked to say.

His mother joined me at a table in the corner of the gift shop. She sat, flashed me a big smile, and waved her husband over. "Ezra! Ivy brought the proofs."

Ezra came and took a seat on my opposite side. The elder McBriars seemed like such nice and easy-going people. I raised my chin as I glanced at Erik. *Close minded jerk,* I thought.

"Okay," I said, handing Diane a sheet with my prices for prints, digital images, and for purchasing images for commercial use. "Now before I show you these, if you don't like them, there's no harm, no foul."

Diane wiggled impatiently in her chair. "You're killing me, girl."

Ezra pulled a pair of reading glasses out of his pocket, slipped them on, and leaned forward. "Let her rip," he said as Erik came over and stood behind him to see the images.

I clicked on the first photo in the cue, and had the supreme satisfaction of hearing Diane gasp. The first images were of Morgan out in the field of holiday trees. A couple were close-ups with Morgan in profile and only the foliage of the evergreens around him. The next several photos showcased the fields of evergreens, with Morgan frolicking in the foreground in his holiday sweater. I had a single shot of him with a serious face, and one of him cheering, from when I'd offered to get him some french fries.

"These are incredible," Ezra said.

"Thank you," I said soberly. I clicked to the next picture and had the pleasure of watching both Ezra and Diane react.

The photo was of Erik. He was walking down the rows of the evergreens. He'd been tugging a pair of work gloves on, and his head was turned slightly away, almost in profile. It was casual, earthy, and natural. I'd played with the colors ever so slightly, and out of curiosity I checked over my shoulder to see his reaction.

Erik was stunned. "I didn't know you'd taken my picture."

"I couldn't resist snapping a candid of you out in the fields," I said, honestly. *I'd never admit to anyone that the man was like a walking advertisement for a modern, rugged farmer. Erik McBriar was the kind of guy they wrote country songs about. The good-looking man who could break your heart without even trying...*

By the goddess, Ivy! I thought to myself. *Pull*

it together, Stop letting your imagination run. Don't blow your big chance.

I clicked forward again and showed them a second shot of Erik. In this photo he was walking past the old, mistletoe-laden apple tree. However, with this photo I had changed from color to a sepia tone.

Diane tapped on the laptop screen. "I want *both* of these photos of Erik."

"Mom," Erik said, sounding embarrassed.

His discomfort absolutely delighted me. It was probably petty, but oh well. I was never going to be a saint.

"I saved the best for last," I said and clicked forward again. The final images were of Morgan and the yellow lab sitting in the pickup bed of the classic red truck, with the weathered tree farm sign in the background.

"My god," Ezra breathed. "That's amazing. It looks like a Christmas card."

I nudged him with an elbow. "I like you, Mr. McBriar."

"Oh, Ivy." Diane was a little teary.

Delighted at her reaction, I followed my instincts and reached over and took her hand. "I thought that one of these photos of Morgan and the dog in the vintage truck would be great advertising for your website, and other social media."

"It's perfect," Diane breathed.

"Also, with your permission," I said. "I've had a request from my friend at the *William's Ford Gazette*. He mentioned to me that he needed a festive photo for Saturday's front page to advertise local small businesses at the holidays." I clicked forward to the image the editor wanted. "This one was his favorite," I said, pointing to the photo of Morgan with his arm around the dog.

"The local paper? Really?" Ezra asked.

"Really," I said, earnestly. "The editor loved the samples I sent him yesterday. You'll need to sign a release form, and the editor has also requested that I take a few more photos of the interior of *Mistletoe Mercantile's* holiday displays. If that's all right with you."

"That would be great!" Ezra said immediately.

"I have the release form for you to sign, right here." I pulled the paper out of my case and set it on the table in front of Ezra. "The editor also said he'd like to use some of the other photos, the ones that I took of your Christmas tree fields on the *Holiday Happenings* website."

"He did?" this was from Erik.

I shifted in my chair to meet his eyes. "Yes. He did. The editor felt it would be a nice boost to tourism and the *Holiday Happenings* event to promote a local Christmas tree farm."

Diane sniffled. "I don't know what to say."

"Oh, and in case you wondered," I told them. "Morgan's parents have given permission for you to use his image in any advertising."

"They don't mind?" Diane asked.

I chuckled. "My entire family is so proud of the pictures of Morgan. Worst case scenario you might have Lexi and Bran bring Belinda out here so I can get her picture in the truck as well."

"Click back one more photo," Diane said.

When I did, she smiled. "That's the one, don't you think, honey?" She looked to her husband.

"Yes," Ezra said. "That's the one we want for our farm's website and social media."

I marked the number. "Okay," I said. "I do have that picture, a social media collage, and a few other photos with my logo watermarked on them if you'd like to purchase a couple now."

"This is going to be *wonderful*!" Diane beamed.

I smiled at her enthusiasm. "If you want to load them up on your social media today, I can email the images to you immediately."

"I'm getting the business checkbook," Diane said, and jumped to her feet.

After I took the interior pictures of the gift shop's displays for the paper, I sat with Diane while she loaded up her favorite watermarked picture of Morgan and Buck in the red pickup to the farm's social media page, and to their *Mistletoe Mercantile* page.

I accepted their check, emailed them the digital images, and promised to have the prints they'd chosen, including both shots of Erik, delivered to them within a week. Finally, I put my laptop away and got ready to go.

Diane and Ezra walked me out and both gave me a hug. "I don't suppose you'd like the job of doing the Santa photos at the farm stand, would you?" Ezra asked.

I cocked my head to the side. "Don't you have someone doing that already?"

Ezra grinned. "It was going to be Ginny's husband taking the photos. We were going to kick it off on Friday evening—St. Nicolas Day. But after seeing what you can do, I think we should up our game and hire a professional."

"What backdrop were you going to use?" I asked.

"Backdrop?" Ezra looked panicked.

I started to laugh. "Don't worry, Mr. McBriar. I think that between Santa, the trees, and that decorated, vintage red truck we're going to be all set."

We chatted over the particulars for a few more moments and then Ezra left to help with a delivery. I was opening my car door to leave when Erik strolled over with a netted four-foot tree balanced on his shoulder. "As requested," he said and began to tie it to the rack on top of my car. "I gave the trunk a fresh cut for you."

My mouth dropped open in shock. "Thanks," I said. "What do I owe you?"

"It's on the house," Erik said.

"That's not necessary," I said, firmly.

Erik kept tying the tree down and never even looked at me as he spoke. "What you are doing for my parents and our farm is worth a hell of a lot more than the price of a spruce."

"Erik, your parents *purchased* those images for their advertising." I put my hands on my hips. "Look, I'm going to get the photo credit and a little publicity as the photographer. The farm gets a boost from public interest and positive PR. It's a win-win. There's no need for this."

Erik stopped and met my eyes from over the roof of the car. The impact from his blue eyes were like a punch to the gut. "You getting our Christmas tree farm featured on the front page of the paper and that holiday tourism website is going to help us out much more than you realize."

"But, I—"

"If we don't have a strong holiday season," he cut me off. "We might have to close down after the first of the year."

"I'm very sorry to hear that," I said, sincerely.

Erik nodded as a reply and finished securing the tree while I waited.

"Thank you for the tree," I said, as he stepped back.

"You're welcome." He gave me the smallest of smiles and walked back inside the farm stand.

His smile had caused my insides to flutter. I wondered over that reaction as I watched him walk away. That smile was one hell of a weapon, I decided. *His butt wasn't bad either.*

Not that it mattered.

I shook my head and climbed in my car. Whether or not he had a great smile and an even greater backside shouldn't have made a damn bit of difference. "It doesn't," I said out loud, if only to make myself feel better about the turn of events. "It *doesn't* matter to me. Not at all."

I smirked, wondering what I was letting myself get so worked up for. He'd probably given me the tree out of guilt, nothing more.

That settled, I cranked up the car radio. *It's The Most Wonderful Time of the Year* was playing and I sang along with Andy Williams on the way home.

***

I snagged Holly as soon as I returned to the manor. “Hey, sis!” I called, slightly out of breath from hauling my camera and laptop bags over one shoulder *and* the tree over the other. I paused at the top of the second flight of steps and tried to catch my breath.

Her long strawberry blonde curls swung as she poked her head out of her bedroom door. “Yeah?”

“Give me a hand with this tree?”

Holly came hustling over and grabbed one end of the wrapped tree before I dropped it. “Good grief, Ivy!”

“Thanks.”

Holly took the laptop case from me and put it over her own shoulder. “How in the world you thought you’d haul all this up to the third-floor by yourself, is beyond me.”

“Determination,” I huffed.

Holly motioned to the attic staircase. “After you.”

"Can I talk to you for a few?" I said after we set the tree down and leaned it against the wall.

"Sure. What's up?" she asked, handing me my laptop case.

I set my equipment on the counter and shut the door behind us so we could have some privacy. "I nabbed a seasonal photography gig today."

"You did?" she smiled. "For the *Holiday Happenings* again?"

"Nope." I shrugged off my vest and hung it on a peg on the back of the door. "Remember how I had that engagement photo shoot at the tree farm?" I gestured for her to go and sit on the couch.

She sat. "Yes, and you took all those cute pictures of Morgan as your test subject."

"Right," I said, sitting beside her. "Well those holiday photos rolled into a bigger opportunity." I said, telling her my news.

I wanted to let her know how things had turned out, and what my plans were for two reasons. One: I might need a few of my shifts covered at the store. And two: I wanted to make sure she wouldn't have her feelings hurt by hearing about me working at the McBriar's tree farm from someone else.

"Ivy." Holly met my eyes. "You don't have to worry. I'm not upset. Diane McBriar is a very nice woman, I like her. I'm happy that your photos will be on the front page of the paper and used in their advertising. That's exciting!"

"There's something else though," I said. "Erik."

Holly shoulders stiffened. "Is he causing problems for you?"

"No," I said. "In fact he's been both civil, and fairly easy to get along with." I quickly filled Holly in on my conversation with Erik, *and* my suggestion to him to do some research on the history of the holiday.

"I would've loved to have seen his face!" Holly threw her head back and started to laugh. "Did he get all pissy after you said that?"

"No." I shook my head. "He was kind of quiet. Then before I left to come home, he gave me the tree—for free. Erik also thanked me for helping his parents, and the tree farm. He was actually *nice* about it all."

"Has he recently sustained a head injury?" she asked with raised eyebrows.

"Not that I was told," I said. "I wanted to talk to you about it, though. I never expected him to be so courteous. Especially to me."

"Yeah, the witchiest Witch in town."

"Exactly." I nodded.

Holly tucked her curls behind an ear. "If I had to hazard a guess, I'd say he learned a hard lesson this summer."

"Yeah. When he shot off his mouth in front of Maggie, his family lost that wedding reception booking because of it. But still, him being so well-mannered—"

"Has put you on edge, eh?" Holly said with a grin.

I blew out a long breath. "Yes, it has."

"You'll be seeing him a lot over the next few weeks," Holly pointed out.

I wrinkled up my nose. "I'll do my best not to zap him in the ass."

Holly snorted with laughter. "Oh, I wish you would. Just once, for me?"

I leaned back against the cushions and studied my sister. She looked good. Happy and healthy, and my intuition told me that she was in love.

"So," I began, "as long as you're in a good mood..."

"I'll cover your shifts at *Enchantments*," Holly said. "You don't have to butter me up."

"Thanks, sis. But I don't want the extra hours interfering with your love life," I said, and watched Holly's smile fade.

I sat back and waited for her to speak. Holly simply folded her arms across her chest and cocked her head to one side. A sure sign that she was annoyed.

"I know you've been seeing someone for a while," I said. "I also know you've been keeping their identity a secret. In fact, you've blocked me so successfully that I can't pick up a thing about them."

"I have my reasons for that," she said.

"Can I ask why you are keeping it a secret?"

She stood. "It's complicated."

"Holly, wait." I reached for her hand. "Your private life is your business. I only wanted to offer my support. I love you and I won't judge. I'd like to meet her."

"Her?" Holly started to chuckle. "Aw hell, Ivy. I'm *not* gay."

Now I stood. "Did you think it would matter to me if you were? You're my sister, my twin. I'm here to support you. I only wanted to make sure that you knew that I love you."

Holly took my hand and gave it a squeeze. "Thanks," she said. "Did you want some help getting that tree decorated?"

She'd changed the subject, so I knew that I wouldn't get anything else out of her. "I could use an extra set of hands getting the tree set up," I admitted.

Holly smiled. "It'll be fun, decorating up here in your new apartment."

"I've got some cool black and white farmhouse decorations for the tree," I said. "Wait until you see."

"Pretty."

"Yeah, it's all black and white plaid and rustic. With pops of red..." I trailed off remembering that I'd purchased a few vintage red farm truck ornaments to go with my Yuletide theme a month ago.

Huh, I thought. *Those ornaments were*

actually very similar to the McBriars' old truck.

I told myself to laugh it off.

But I did wonder over the synchronicity.

CHAPTER SIX

On a quick hunch, I made a pit stop before arriving at the farm the next afternoon. I had stopped and purchased a trio of holiday pillows, colored LED lights, batteries, and a festive blanket to add to my bag of props. I also picked up something else, dog treats. The compulsion to buy them was so strong that I followed my intuition and added them to my other purchases.

"Here we go," I told myself, as I pulled my car around to the back parking lot as Ezra McBriar had suggested. The holiday photo sessions were scheduled to begin at 4:00 pm and I was looking forward to getting started.

I'd hitched my camera bag over my shoulder and started to pick up the huge bag of props when Diane hailed me.

"Ivy!" she called.

I waved. "Hey, Diane."

She came hustling over, and the closer she came the more I realized something was wrong.

"We had a bit of vandalism last night," she said, before I could ask. "We've been working all day to put things back into place, and to repair the damage."

"Damage?" I asked. "What happened? Everything looks fine to me."

"Wreaths were ripped up, trees torn apart. They pulled the lights and pine roping down, and tried to break in the door to the gift shop." Her hands waved in the air. "Then Mr. Jensen called and said he has the flu! What are we going to do without a Santa for the Santa photos? I can't believe this happened on the *day before* we're scheduled to be featured in the newspaper!"

"I'm sorry to hear that Mr. Jensen is sick," I said. "You reported the vandalism, right?" I asked.

"Yes. First thing this morning. The police said it was malicious mischief." Diane tugged a knit hat further down over her hair. "Ezra spent all morning installing security cameras. My daughter Ginny, and her husband Gary went out and replaced the Christmas lights, and they both stayed and helped me rehang all the lights with fresh pine roping. My mother has been in the gift shop all day, trying to help. Thankfully, Erik repaired the shop door, and the staff helped clean up the mess."

"I'm sorry, Diane. Is there something you'd like me to do?"

She steered me around to the front of the barn. "I could use some fresh eyes for a start," she said. "How does it all look now?"

I saw that a few things had been rearranged. Now red lights were strung in with the greenery instead of white, but other than that... "It looks good to me. Really great."

"I'm too stressed to see it clearly anymore," Diane said. "But what will we do without a Santa for the pictures?"

"I have a hunch all we'll need is your old red truck," I said. "It wasn't damaged during the vandalism was it?"

"No!" Diane shuddered. "Thank god we had that classic truck locked up in the garage."

Even as she spoke, Ezra drove it up to the front of the barn.

He parked in the spot we'd chosen the day before, pocketed the keys, and walked over. "We made it!" he said, with a grin to Diane. "All ready to go for the big holiday kick off, tonight."

"Diane was telling me that you've had a little excitement," I said.

Ezra rolled his eyes. "Probably a bunch of kids looking to cause trouble. I'm thankful it wasn't any worse."

An elderly woman with white hair and a Nordic sweater stepped out of the gift shop. "I told you," she said, "it was the Yule lads."

Diane shut her eyes. "Mom, please."

"The Yule lads?" I smiled at the elderly woman. "I thought that was an Icelandic tradition?"

My question earned me a beaming smile. "The Yule lads are pranksters. They are Yuletide tricksters known throughout Scandinavia," she said. "Did you know that Iceland was once ruled by Norway and then the Danes? Danish is still the second most common language in Iceland."

"Here we go," Diane sighed.

I grinned, absolutely charmed by the woman. "Hi, I'm Ivy Bishop." I stuck out my hand.

"Greta Larson," she introduced herself. "I am the mother of the woman currently rolling her eyes at me."

Diane *was* rolling her eyes, and caught, she started to laugh. "Come on, Mom. We need to set up the hot chocolate bar. You can tell Ivy all about Scandinavian Christmas folklore later this weekend."

"Be sure that I will." Greta nodded to me.

"I'll look forward to that." I smiled at Greta.

"Excuse us." Diane and her mother went back into the gift shop, leaving me with Mr. McBriar.

"I'm sorry to ask after everything you went through today," I said. "Do you still have those items we talked about? The wooden sled and your vintage sign?"

Ezra nodded. "I do. The sign is lying flat in the bed of the truck and the sled is in the gift shop. Did you need any help getting ready for the photos?"

"Tell you what? Why don't you leave that to me, you have enough to do. I'll get the truck staged and ready."

"This wasn't quite the image we'd hope to project," Ezra said, dipping his hands in his coat pockets.

I laid a supportive hand on his coat sleeve. "You mean the strong family who dives in and all works together to overcome an obstacle?"

"We've had some bad luck this past year," Ezra said. "But I like the way you put it—the working together—I like that much better."

"Don't you worry, Mr. McBriar," I said. "Your luck is already changing. When that photo of Morgan in that classic red truck hits the front page tomorrow, your weekend sales will be epic."

"We spent a lot of money getting ready for this season," he said. "I sure hope so."

"I know so." I nodded.

His walkie-talkie squawked. "Erik is bringing up a batch of fresh cuts to fill up the racks," he said.

I nodded. "Sounds good."

He flashed a quick smile and was off,

speaking in the walkie and moving across the parking lot.

As soon as he left, I went to work. The area we'd chosen for the photos was between the far corner of *Mistletoe Mercantile* and one end of the racks where the pre-cut trees were displayed. At the moment those racks were empty, which made me wonder how many trees they'd lost due to the vandalism.

I pulled the strands of battery-operated LED holiday lights out of my prop bag and dropped the tailgate. Climbing up, I set about re-staging the truck bed for the photos. I added lights to the fresh wreath and stood the sign back up. I fluffed the pine boughs, shook out the plaid wool blanket, and added in the holiday theme pillows I'd brought along. Finally, I draped the new fleece buffalo plaid blanket over the edge of the tailgate.

With a grunt I swung over the side, dropped to the gravel, and headed inside the gift shop to retrieve that vintage wooden sled. The one I'd spied that had fresh greenery and old rusty bells. I was carting it back outside when I saw that Erik and an employee were filling up the tree racks.

I leaned the sled against the open tailgate, stood back and made a few adjustments to the blanket. A cold canine nose pressed against my hand, and I glanced down to discover Buck, the yellow lab, standing beside me.

"Hi ya, Buck." I reached over and scratched his ears. In response he collapsed to the gravel and rolled over to expose his belly. "Oh, poor puppy. Doesn't anyone give you any love?" I said sympathetically, and bent over and gave him a belly rub.

"Now you've done it," Erik said. "He'll follow you everywhere."

I smiled over my shoulder. "He's a great dog." With a final pat, I stood and regarded Erik. "Your folks were telling me about the vandalism last night. You guys must have worked your asses off today, because everything looks great now."

"Thanks." Erik nodded. "What are you going to do without a Santa for your pictures?" he asked.

"Improvise, adapt and overcome," I said. "Don't worry, I have a few tricks up my sleeves."

Erik studied me carefully. "Well," he said after a long moment. "I better get back to filling up the tree racks. I'll be nearby tonight if you have any problems."

He was going to be keeping an eye on me, I realized. Erik was still a tad nervous due to my presence at the farm, and I imagined that he still felt the need to protect his family from the likes of witchy little old me.

"Okay. See ya, boss." I gave him a sassy salute and turned my attention back to the truck.

Buck rolled to his feet and stood in front of me, wagging his tail.

"Buck." I said his name softly. "How would you like to be in the holiday photos?"

Buck barked and his tongue rolled out happily.

Checking to make sure Erik was gone, I bent down, and took a hold of the yellow lab's head with both hands. "Buck, you're a good dog both loyal and true; help me out tonight as we have work to do."

The dog held completely still, his eyes

locked on mine, as I finished the spell in a whispered voice. "Hear my voice and heed my call, be friendly and charming to one and all. By the powers of earth, sky, and sea, as I will it, so mote it be."

I let go of the dog and gave him a pat on the head. Reaching in my pocket, I pulled out the doggy treats I'd spontaneously purchased an hour ago. "Partners." I held one up. "Right, buddy?"

Buck sat and I gave him the treat. As if to seal the deal, Buck lifted a paw to shake.

My instincts were right on the money. No Santa was necessary. People were *thrilled* with the opportunity to pose in the decorated, classic truck with the Christmas trees in the background. As soon as night fell, I clicked on the lights I'd wrapped around the wreath and it all looked magickal.

Buck was delighted at all the attention and petting, and pretty much stole the show. He sat with the families, laid with his head in a few elementary aged boys' laps and was a superstar. In my prop bag I also had fur trimmed Santa hats for folks who wanted to use them, and red knit scarves to borrow. They added a festive touch to any outfit if needed—I also had a box of miniature candy canes for bribing the kids into posing.

The classic truck captured the adult's imagination, while the dog and the candy made it an enjoyable experience for the kids. However, it wasn't only families and kids that I'd photographed, it was also couples. Many of whom wanted to use the picture for their Christmas cards.

While the holiday music played over the loudspeakers, the McBriars sold trees, wreaths, and fresh evergreen roping. Diane was rocking the gift shop. Greta served up hot chocolate, and Ezra and Erik continuously loaded up fresh holiday trees for their customers, while the staff hauled folks who wanted to cut their own back and forth to the tree fields.

I took over a dozen sets of photos, accepted payments with my card reader on my smart phone, and passed out claim tickets for the digital images. I was very pleased with the sales I'd had for my first night. I imagined the farm's fifteen percent cut might even help them out a little.

As I scrolled through the images I'd captured, I decided to print up a price sheet for fifteen minute holiday-truck mini photography sessions, as soon as I arrived home. I would hand those out—starting tomorrow. I would use the images of Morgan and Buck and make a collage. Trim out the flyer and the prices with red lettering. It would look super slick. I'd also add that picture collage/price sheet to the homepage on my personal photography website and social media page as well.

I had a strong gut hunch that I would be able to snag a few more engagement photo shoots, and maybe even a wedding next year, with the publicity I could garner from these mini holiday photo sessions at the farm. Once my photo of Morgan and the dog in the classic red truck hit the front page of the paper in the morning it'd be crazy busy.

I could hardly wait.

***

The first Saturday in December dawned with

temperatures in the 40's and partly cloudy skies. According to the McBriars, the first weekend in December was prime tree shopping time. I'd been woken up at 5:00 am by a very excited Diane McBriar. Their phone had been ringing off the hook in reaction to their farm being featured in the paper and the William's Ford tourism website. Folks were asking lots of questions about the tree farm, the gift shop, and the photo opportunities.

Diane was calling out even more help, as they were expecting to be swamped. I had already planned on being there by eight—as they opened at nine—but now Diane wanted to know if I could come at 7:30 instead, with the rest of the staff.

Her enthusiasm was contagious, and for once I didn't mind being up early at all. I rolled out of bed, hit the shower and got dressed.

I was buttoning up a heavy black denim shirt over a thermal long-sleeved t-shirt when my cell signaled that I had a text message. I saw that it was from Eddie O'Connell. He'd asked if I'd learned anything new about the creature that had attacked him and his friends.

I texted back that I had been researching, but hadn't learned anything new yet. I told him I would be out at the tree farm for most of the weekend for a photography gig.

My phone rang. It was Eddie, so I answered. "Hey, Eddie."

"Did you talk to Erik?"

"Briefly," I said. "I do know that the McBriars and their staff are taking this seriously. I've been trying to find the right time to ask what exactly happened to their dog, all I know for sure is that it didn't make it. But I haven't learned anything else."

Eddie sighed. "Okay, be careful out there."

"I will. Don't you worry," I promised.

"See ya," Eddie said and hung up.

I finished getting ready for the day, gathered up the equipment I'd readied the night before and headed out.

I pulled my car over to the side of the road behind a half dozen other cars waiting to be let into the farm's gate. I lifted a hand in greeting to one of the ladies who worked in the gift shop and a couple of minutes later, a gator vehicle came zipping down the farm road.

Erik McBriar hopped out and went to unlock the heavy-duty metal gate. *Metal,* I noted. I suppose they upgraded after Maggie had driven straight through their fancy wooden gate a few months ago while rescuing Willow.

I followed the other employees up the drive and parked in our designated area. I gathered all the things I would need for the day, my zippered laptop case, camera bag, tripod and the prop bag. I shifted the load, left my lunch in the car, and locked it up.

I barely entered the back door to the retail area when I was swooped into a big hug by Diane McBriar.

"Ivy!" She ignored all the equipment I carried, and pressed a kiss to my cheek. "The photos of the tree farm and gift shop looks fantastic on the website, and I still can't believe that we actually were featured on the front page of the paper!"

She steered me inside the gift shop, and Ezra grinned, and waved a copy of the paper at me. I was turning to go out front, and saw that Erik was standing behind the counter, speaking on the phone. He nodded in recognition and smiled at me.

A big, full, honest grin that completely changed Erik McBriar's face.

I blinked at the sudden alteration to his appearance. The smile did wonders for him. He'd always been nice-looking, but now that he was genuinely happy, it bumped him up to smoking hot.

Don't even go there, I warned myself. *He might be attractive, but that didn't make him any more open-minded.*

Diane put the front page of the paper on the wall. She and Ezra used tape to hold it up behind the checkout counter, and Greta suggested they have it framed. While the staff had a quick meeting, I ducked out to begin setting up for the photos. It was then that I discovered that Diane had added a vintage wooden card table and a pair of rustic Windsor chairs for me to use as a workstation.

The improvements would come in damn handy while I filled out claim checks and passed out my fancy new price sheets. I pulled the new flyers out of my laptop bag, set my camera bag on top of them and rested the prop bag on a chair. Ezra drove his truck slowly around to the front of the barn. He parked it in the designated spot, and I set to work, freshening up the display in the truck bed.

Right before the gates opened, I snagged Erik. "Tell your mom thanks for setting up the table and chairs. Having it will make it much easier to work today."

"Mom didn't set it up," Erik said. "I did."

"Oh." I cleared my throat. "Well, that was nice of you."

"I saw how busy you were last night, and figured the table would be more convenient than trying to use your laptop perched on the front seat of the truck."

So he *had* been keeping an eye on me yesterday. To try and put him at ease, I sent him a friendly smile. "The table will be much more efficient," I said. "Thanks, Erik."

"If you need anything, pop in the gift shop or give a call on the walkie." He pulled one off his belt and handed it to me.

"Great," I said, clipping it to the waist of my jeans as I'd seen the rest of the staff do. "Thanks again."

"I have to go open the gates. We're going to be crazy busy by noon, so if you need a break, take one. If you need some help, be sure and let someone know."

"Got it," I said with a nod. Erik swung into one of the gators and headed out to go and open the gate.

Alone for the moment, I took a deep breath, connected to the earth and said a prayer. I asked the goddess to bless the farm with prosperity, and to keep my creativity flowing for what would surely be a very long day. I took a seat at the table and started to organize my equipment and paperwork, as the very first customers of the day rolled into the Christmas tree farm.

I'd been working for maybe an hour when a familiar voice called my name.

"Hi, Ivy!"

I turned to see young Charlie Bell running full out. She was dressed in a hunter green coat and wore a bright red hat and scarf.

"Hi, kiddo." I reached down and gave her a one-armed hug and saw over her head that her father Matthew and his fiancée Violet O'Connell were walking toward me.

"Hey, Violet." I smiled at our family friend. I nodded to her fiancé. "Matthew."

"We came to get a tree!" Charlie announced.

I nodded. "This is the place for it."

"I needed to pick up some more fresh evergreen for the florist shop as well," Violet added.

Charlie tugged on my insulated vest. "Violet showed me the picture you took of Morgan in the red truck. It was in the paper this morning."

Matthew admired the classic red truck. "Wow, that's an awesome vintage truck."

"It is, isn't it?" I agreed.

"Where's the dog?" Charlie wanted to know.

"Buck's around here somewhere, greeting folks," I said to Charlie. "It's his job."

Charlie's eyes were huge. "The dog has a job?"

Before I could respond, a loud whistle pierced the air. I looked automatically and discovered that Erik was in the lot and had whistled for the dog.

Buck trotted to him, and Erik brought the dog over. "More of Buck's fan club have arrived?" he asked, with a smile to the girl.

"He's really big," Charlie said, reaching back uncertainly for her father's hand.

"Buck," Erik said. "Show your manners to the ladies."

Buck plopped his rump down in front of Charlie and lifted a paw to shake.

Charlie started to giggle and accepted the canine handshake.

"This is a great dog," Violet said, ruffling the lab's ears.

"Would you like to have your picture taken with Buck?" I asked Charlie.

"Can I, Daddy?" Charlie asked Matthew. "Can I?"

Matthew smiled. "Of course you can, honey."

"Buck," I called to the dog and patted the tailgate. "Come on up."

The yellow lab leapt nimbly in the back of the pickup with hardly any encouragement, and sat. I gave him a dog treat from a bag in my pocket and he looked at me adoringly.

I was going to reach for Charlie, but before I could, Erik picked her up under her arms swung her high, then set a laughing Charlie in place.

Erik moved immediately back and I picked up the camera from where it hung around my neck and quickly took a few pictures.

"Why don't we get some family photos?" I said to Matthew and Violet a few moments later. "Buck." I snapped my fingers, pointed to the ground and the yellow lab jumped out and sat beside me. While Matthew and Violet joined Charlie on the tailgate of the truck, I slipped the dog a treat.

"Oh, *that's* why he likes you," Erik chuckled. "You've been bribing him."

"Rewarding," I corrected as the dog leaned against my legs. "Rewarding an animal is an effective method in training."

"I thought maybe," Erik said, very softly, "that you were using magick."

CHAPTER SEVEN

"Not at the moment, I'm not," I said, honestly.

"But you do," he said very softly. "Use magick."

I raised an eyebrow at him. "Yes, and on a fairly regular basis, as a matter of fact."

He kept his voice low. "I see."

"I understand that you had a bad experience with your ex and her hiring someone to cast spells on you," I said. "But that's *not* my style, Erik."

"That's good to know," he said, without rancor. "The whole subject makes me nervous."

I shifted my eyes up to meet his. "It shouldn't. Most practitioners adhere to a strict code of ethical behavior."

"They do?" he asked.

Since his tone had been genuine and not snide, I answered him. "Yes, we do," I said. "But magickal ethics is not something I can explain in thirty seconds or less."

"And this isn't the time or place to get into that." He nodded.

"No it's not," I agreed.

"We're ready, Ivy," Violet called over.

"I'll be right there," I answered her.

"Sorry. I'll let you get back to work," Erik said. He gave a wave to the Bells and walked away.

I shifted my focus back on the family of three that were waiting for my attention. I made a few corrections to how they were sitting, stepped back, framed them in, and shot a quick half dozen of casual photos.

Afterward, Violet and I were seated at the table, while the lab sprawled out beneath it. Matthew stood behind her, and they viewed the photos together. Writing down the lot number on her claim check, I took her payment and filled out her receipt. "Your photos will be online and available for download later tonight."

I expected that the family would leave to go and purchase their tree and greenery now that we were finished, but instead, Violet leaned back in her chair.

"See?" Violet smiled up at Matthew. "I told you."

Matthew grinned. "You were right, absolutely."

"What's going on?" I asked the couple.

"Matthew and I were wondering if you would do us a huge favor," Violet said. "Our wedding photographer had a conflict with his schedule and has cancelled on us."

"A month before your wedding?" I was horrified.

"He suggested a replacement, but I didn't care for their style, or the bump in price," Violet admitted.

"And you'd like me to suggest someone else?"

"No." Violet laid her hand on top of mine. "We'd like *you* to photograph our wedding."

A solo gig, I thought to myself. *Oh my goddess!* I struggled not to bounce in my chair.

"I'd be honored to photograph your wedding," I said formally to the couple.

Violet blew out a long relieved breath. "Thank you."

"No. Thank you!" I couldn't help it, I reached over and grabbed her up in a hug. "I'm going to take the best wedding photos you have ever had!"

Violet grinned. "We can talk particulars in a couple of days."

"Of course!" I agreed. "I'm going to want to see your dress. We should talk about your décor and flowers, so I can get a feel for the theme and tone you want for the big day."

"Wow," Matthew said. "Our original photographer never even asked us about any of that."

I let go of Violet and jumped up to hug Matthew as well. "Thank you for trusting me with this."

"Daddy!" Charlie said, impatiently. "Can we go get some hot chocolate now?"

"Go," I said to the Bells. "Go get your tree, and there *is* a hot chocolate bar inside the gift shop."

"Do they have marshmallows?" Charlie asked suspiciously.

"I'm pretty sure they do." I told the girl.

The family headed inside to go check out the hot chocolate, and my head was spinning with ideas for shooting Violet and Matthew's winter wedding.

I felt Buck press his nose against my fingers and I reached down to pat his head. "What do you think about that, Buck?" I gave his ears a scratch. "I mean, I'd hoped to get some wedding clients on my own at *some* point in the near future. But this?"

The lab gave a soft *woof* as a reply, and as soon I dropped back down in the chair, he laid his head in my lap. I sat there for a few moments, thrilled with this new opportunity. Violet's request had been a terrific surprise. Suddenly, out of my peripheral, I saw a couple approach the table.

"Are you the photographer?" they asked.

"That would be me." I smiled and rose to my feet.

"We would like our picture taken. Together." They added the last, and I focused fully on them. The two young women stood hand in hand. Both were in head to toe black, and had a trendy sort of punk-hipster look about them.

"Of course." I smiled at them. "Wow! I *love* your hair," I said to the shorter of the two, who had purple and blue dreads and was wearing trendy glasses.

"Thank you." She smiled. "I'm Alison, and this is my partner, Janie. We saw that picture in the paper, and really liked the red truck with the trees in the background."

"It's nice to meet you." I reached out and shook their hands. "Did you want to be casually seated in the back of the truck bed? Or would you prefer something more romantic, like standing with your arms around each other and leaning against the truck's door?"

"What do you think, babe?" Janie asked Alison.

"Tell you what," I said. "I'll try a couple of different poses." I got the couple in position. "I did an engagement photo shoot with a couple the other day," I said, while I checked the camera settings. "We used this truck as a prop. Their photos turned out great."

"Actually..." Alison grinned and flashed a ring. "We recently got engaged."

"Congratulations!" I said automatically.

"What's this I hear about an engagement, Alison?" Diane McBriar walked up to join us, and she moved directly to hug the young woman. "That's so exciting!"

"Janie," Alison said after the hug. "Meet Diane McBriar. Her family owns the farm."

"Hello." Janie smiled shyly.

"I went to college with Erik," Alison explained.

"That's cool," I said.

"And I've interrupted," Diane laughed. "Sorry."

"That's okay." I smiled.

"Is it all right if I hang around for a few, and watch?" Diane wanted to know.

"Sure," I said. "I don't mind."

I pulled a red plaid scarf from the prop bag, and added it around Janie's neck, and re-posed the couple again. "Okay, you two look at each other now." When they did, they both started to smile, and Janie blushed. I took several photos in quick succession. I paused, checked the digital screen and started to grin. *Damn,* I thought, stopping on my favorite. *That's a keeper.*

Diane peered over my shoulder at the image. "Oh," she breathed. "That's adorable."

"Can we see?" Janie asked.

"Of course." I took the memory card out of the camera and loaded it in the laptop. While I scrolled past the pictures of the Bells, Diane was chatting up the couple.

Alison and Janie were so happy with their holiday pictures that they decided they wanted one to be their engagement photo. I slipped the price list for prints to the couple, gave them their claim ticket, and told them the digital images would be online tonight.

"You can accept payment over your website, right?" Janie asked.

"I sure can."

"Do you have a portfolio of wedding photography?" Janie asked me, setting the scarf back on the table.

"I will by the end of January," I said, trying not to grin like a lunatic. "My website address is on the price sheet I gave your fiancée. You can check out some of my other work there."

"I think we'll do that tonight," Janie said.

Erik walked by, carrying a tree over his shoulder. He glanced my way and stopped. "Alison?" he asked.

"Erik!" She jumped to her feet and raced to him. "I was hoping we'd see you today!" She hugged him, tree and all.

Erik balanced the tree on his shoulder and hugged her back every bit as hard as she had him. "Did you come out to get your Christmas tree?"

"Of course." She smiled. "Who else would we buy it from?"

I sat back in my chair and watched as Alison introduced Erik to her fiancée. The three of them wandered off chatting away, and I slid my eyes over to Diane. "Is your wedding venue still open?"

"Yes," Diane said. "But we haven't had any bookings in months."

I gave her an elbow nudge. "I bet if you mention to the brides that you have a venue available, they'd book it."

"Do you think so?" Diane's voice trailed off

as she thought it over.

“Call it a hunch,” I said. “Be sure to remind them of me, when they start talking about choosing a photographer for their big day.”

“You bet.” Diane started to grin. “Oh look, they went inside the gift shop with Erik.”

“Well, if I were you, I’d get those girls some free hot chocolate and go schmooze.”

“Good idea,” Diane said and was off like a shot.

***

The rest of the day passed in a whirl. I remembered to take a lunch break only because Greta Larson showed up to my table with a mug of hot chocolate and a sandwich. I tried to tell her I’d brought a lunch, but she waved that away, sat with me and told me she wasn’t leaving until I ate something.

“I knew your mother,” she said.

“You did?” I said over a mouthful of sandwich.

“Yes, I was very sorry for your family when she passed.”

I worked hard to keep a smile on my face. My mother had died when I'd been in high school, it was never easy to talk or think about that. But it was easy to remember the good times and I was grateful that I'd had her to teach me the Craft.

Greta patted my shoulder in sympathy, and I forced myself to keep a smile in place. I found it wasn't hard, as the woman had her white hair up in a bun, and between her Nordic reindeer sweater, pretty plump face, and kindness, she made me think of Mrs. Claus.

The turkey sandwich she'd made was wonderful and the hot chocolate was the best I'd ever had. I ate quickly and was thoroughly entertained by Greta's creepy stories about the Scandinavian spirits of Yuletide.

After I finished my sandwich, she patted me on the head and took the plate back. I was told to call her, 'Grandma Larson', as all the other employees did, and then she went inside to run the hot chocolate bar.

I was excited to discover that there were plenty of folks wanting their picture taken, *and* the mini sessions I offered were very popular. I probably should have charged a tad more. But a girl has to start somewhere. I stayed so busy that I filled up one memory card and started a second.

Ginny, Erik's sister, brought her brood by, and I did a mini photo session for them as well. Erik showed up at the end of it, and the three kids promptly lost their minds and dove on him, demanding to be taken on a ride around the farm. I smiled when I watched him scoop up all three kids and cart them off. He loaded them up in a gator and they took off laughing across the tree fields.

At six o'clock Diane rounded me up, insisting I take my break. She had some exciting news to share as we stored my equipment away. It seemed like Alison and Janie *were* very interested in booking the barn for their wedding ceremony and reception in a few months. They'd even gone so far as to put a small deposit down to hold the date.

"Things are actually looking up for us!" she said. "It was those photos of Morgan and Buck that got the ball rolling." Diane steered me to the back of the gift shop. "You got your first chance at photographing a wedding on your own. People are excited to visit the Christmas tree farm, and now, we have our first wedding booking at the barn in almost six months. It's like magick!"

"Tis the season." I gave her a wink, and she threw back her head and laughed.

I was told to take a half hour off, and I didn't argue. In the employee room, there were several crockpots filled with chili and they smelled fantastic. Gratefully, I got a bowl and helped myself.

It felt good to be out of the cold. I pulled up a chair, happy to warm up, and sat at a long table next to Ezra who was crushing crackers all over the last of his chili.

"There she is!" Ezra said over a mouthful of chili. "Diane told me about the wedding barn booking."

"It's wonderful news," I agreed.

"Ivy, you have some kind of magick," Ezra said, pulling out another sleeve of saltines. "Since you came here everything has started to change, for the better."

"A girl does what she can," I said, and had

Ezra hooting with laughter. I waited a beat. "Did you leave me any crackers?" I asked him.

"Dad, I never could understand why you'd ruin perfectly good chili with all those crackers." This came from Erik, who'd walked in the room.

I jolted at the sound of Erik's voice. I knew he'd overheard what his father had said, and I wondered how he'd react. I decided to try a little humor. "Crackers are meant to be put on chili," I said, sticking my nose in the air. "Clearly, Erik, you have no taste."

"That is just so *wrong*," Erik said, shaking his head.

"Big talk from the guy who covers his chili with cheese," Ezra said to his son.

"Is there cheese?" I asked. "I didn't see any."

"Hang on," Erik said, and he went to the table with the crockpots, picked up a bag of shredded cheese, and passed it to me.

"Yum," I said, and sprinkled a handful on top my chili as well.

Ezra finished his bowl and stood. I was surprised when Erik sat down in the space his father had vacated. It was disconcerting to realize that the other staff members were leaving too. Their dinner break was over, which meant I was alone. With Erik McBriar.

"Alison and Janie were thrilled with your pictures," Erik said after a moment.

"They're a super-cute couple." I took a bite of chili and congratulated myself on making pleasant dinner conversation. "Alison said you were friends in college?"

Erik scooped up his chili. "We were. She has a degree in organic agriculture. We ended up having a lot of Agro classes together.'

"Agro?" I asked.

"Agricultural Sciences," he explained.

I nodded and got up to get myself a can of soda.

"Mom told me that Violet O'Connell asked you to take her wedding photos next month," he said, as soon as I sat back down.

"Yes, she did." I had a moment to regret that I'd bubbled over about my big news to Diane earlier, but I'd been so excited. "Their photographer cancelled out on them, and I got lucky."

"I had a chance to check out a few of the

images you pulled up on your laptop for the customers off and on today," Erik said. "It's not luck. You're incredibly talented, Ivy."

My breath huffed out. "Thank you," I said cautiously.

Erik lifted his brows. "You sound surprised at the compliment."

"Let's say that I'm surprised to have received a genuine compliment from you." I took a steadying breath before continuing. "You told me the subject of magick makes you nervous, and it's pretty common knowledge how you feel about my family."

"I watched you today," Erik said. "People like you. Kids especially. My parents think you're great. Buck follows you around constantly, and it's not because you gave him treats."

"Okay," I said, not sure where he was headed with this.

"Those twin boys you photographed right after lunch?" Erik shifted to face me.

I thought back. "Oh sure, the Davis twins." The two-year-old brothers had been a bit of a challenge but I'd still managed to get some cute photos.

"Those kids were on the edge of a meltdown, their parents were stressed out…and then you picked up one of those boys, whispered something to him, and he stopped crying instantly."

I had sent calming energy to that two-year-old. But I hadn't realized anyone else had caught on to that. *He'd been watching me more closely than I'd imagined.*

Deliberately, I chose my next words with care. "I live in the same house with my niece and nephew. I've had some practice with calming cranky kids."

"Yeah, and I've spent enough time babysitting my sister's brood to know that a kid that age *isn't* easy to handle." He sat back in his chair. "So is what you did, like a Witch thing? I saw Holly do something similar for my nephew, George, when he was a baby."

I checked to make sure we were still alone in the break room. "A Witch thing? Yes and no. A talented energy worker could pass along healing, calming, or supportive vibrations to another." I leaned my arms on the table as I spoke. “Honestly Erik, it depends on the particular Witch’s talents as to how successful they are with clairsentience—that’s the technical term for psychic empathy,” I explained.

“I know what psychic empathy is,” Erik said. “It’s feeling another’s emotions as if they were you own.”

“Exactly.” I nodded. “Now, not all empaths can *push* their emotions to another person. Some empaths are easily overwhelmed by all the emotions they can sense from other people. Which means that they have to work at it to protect themselves.”

Erik nodded. “Go on.”

“Then there are those extremely sensitive psychic empaths that experience negative emotions from others to an extent that it causes them actual pain.”

“Jesus.” Erik’s eyes grew wide.

“For example,” I said. “My sister, Holly is such an empath. And if she has negative feelings such as anger, distrust, or hatred directed at her, it’s as physically painful as a sucker-punch to the gut.”

"I had no idea." Erik sounded more than a little horrified. "Are you an empath too?"

"My talents are more concentrated around my intuition, and a few other magickal abilities."

"So to be clear," Erik said, dragging a hand through his hair, "that day when I spoke to Holly about her leaving the antique shop, and because I was angry, I might have caused her physical pain?"

And the light dawns, I thought. "That would be correct."

"Oh god," Erik said in a shaky voice. "I had no idea."

I watched him closely. His pupils had dilated, and a blush rode his cheeks. Physical clues that he was both embarrassed and upset by the information. "It was a long time ago, Erik," I said. "And fortunately for you, Holly doesn't hold much of a grudge."

"But you do," Erik said.

"You hurt my sister," I said levelly. "Whether by accident or design you caused her pain when her resistance was low because she was recovering from an attack."

Erik narrowed his eyes. “So not only was she physically hurt during the break-in, but she was injured on a psychic level as well?”

“Yes.” I left it at that. Otherwise he might discover that we’d known all along who the assailant had been.

“When I found out what Raelynn had done,” Erik said, checking to make sure we were still alone. “That my fiancée had paid someone to cast spells on me, so I’d fall in line with her plans. I was angry, but I was also freaked out.”

“That’s understandable,” I said. “No one likes to think their romantic feelings are being controlled by another. For a mundane who is already uncomfortable with the idea of magick, I would imagine you were especially angry.”

“For a long time, I was,” Erik admitted with a sigh.

“You should know that manipulating another’s emotions is considered to be about as low as you can go in the Witch community,” I said. “Giving someone a tiny boost to be more courageous, or sending a fussy child some serenity is one thing. Messing with a person’s free will is altogether different.”

"So there are rules."

"And consequences when they are broken." I smoothed back my hair. "As your ex-fiancée discovered."

Erik's jaw dropped. "So you're saying that Raelynn's car accident, and lapsed insurance that became huge legal problems was a sort of pay back for what she did to me?"

"There's no 'sort of' about it. Karma's a bitch," I said, sweetly.

Erik did a double-take. "Whoa."

"There's something else you should know," I said. "It was Holly and my Aunt Faye who worked the magick that broke the spells that had been cast on you."

He frowned over that. "They did?"

"Of course. Holly would never leave someone—not even you—to suffer that way."

Erik sat there, silently studying me. It was almost as if he'd never seen me before.

I checked the clock on the wall. My break was almost up. I stood and picked up my soda and empty bowl.

"Ivy," Erik stopped me by touching my arm.

"Yes?"

"Thank you for telling me," he said. "You've given me a lot to think about."

"Witches are *not* the bad guys, Erik," I said. "Someday, I hope that you will come to understand that." I went to put my paper bowl in the trash.

"Can I ask you one more thing before you go?"

I stopped at the doorway. "You may ask."

"What is *your* magickal specialty?'

"Maybe someday, I'll show you." I met his eyes and smiled. "That is, when I think you can handle it."

CHAPTER EIGHT

I woke up Sunday morning, staggered over to my desk, and checked my website to see how my online sales had been. I pulled up the page and did such a hard double-take that I literally fell out of my chair.

"Ouch!" I rubbed my hip and started to laugh. I climbed to my feet, checked the totals again, and gave myself a moment to let it all sink in. The online sales I'd accrued overnight were *much* better than I'd imagined. "Damn, Skippy!"

I danced over to my mini fridge and grabbed a soda—my only choice for caffeine in the morning—and went back to my desk.

Since I had a very limited window of opportunity for the holiday photos, I had worked until two in the morning, tweaking and polishing the images for the customers that had ordered prints yesterday. I had emailed my order in and would pick them up from the printer Monday afternoon.

Now I had *another* list of online orders for prints, and I would need to get those going tonight. The next few weeks were going to be crazy busy with very long hours. It would be best if I made myself a work list for later this evening, I decided. I grabbed a pad of paper and wrote it all down. Once that was done, I leaned back and stretched my arms over my head.

I remembered to check the weather forecast, and saw that we had a chance for light snow today. That meant I would need to switch to heavier outer gear *and* figure out how to weatherproof my outdoor table and workspace. Worst case scenario I might have to put that table and chairs in the gift shop, to protect my equipment.

I'd figure it out once I got to the farm, I decided. Now, I had about an hour to get ready for another full day of photography.

When I arrived, I discovered that the McBriars had a plan for the weather. They'd pitched a pop-up canopy over my table and chairs. Ezra had fastened tarps to three of its sides, and Diane was on a stepstool, hanging a wreath on the front of the pop-up as I prepped for the day.

"Now you are all set!" She clicked on the battery-operated lights and hopped down.

Not only was the arrangement cute, but it would also keep me, my laptop, and the paperwork out of the wind and the wet. Good thing too, as Sunday brought a brisk business, and a series of snow showers, which added to the Yuletide atmosphere.

It was much colder today, and I had added a Santa hat trimmed out in black fur to my outfit and was wearing my heaviest black coat. However, the temperatures didn't slow down the tree shoppers and the folks who wanted their photos taken. If anything, the dusting of snow only made it more festive.

I took a break to warm up in the gift shop, and was standing sipping a hot chocolate with Grandma Larson when I spotted Eddie

O'Connell with his brother Kevin and their dad, Carl, in the shop.

I waved. "Hello, O'Connell family!"

Kevin was all smiles, Carl was cheerful, and Eddie stood there looking miserable.

Carl and Kevin basically ignored Eddie's behavior and went to go pay for their chosen fresh-cut tree. As soon as they moved off, Eddie asked if he could speak to me privately.

I noticed the break room was empty, so I grabbed his jacket sleeve and tugged him in there. "What's happened?"

"I wondered if you'd heard anything new. Anything at all about the monster in the woods?"

"I talked to Ezra McBriar the other day," I said quietly. "They believe the dog they lost was due to coyotes, or maybe a random bobcat."

"Shit." Eddie scowled.

"I'm trying to be as discreet as possible," I hissed. "It won't do either of us any good if we go around asking folks if they've seen a monster in the woods."

"So what do we do now?"

"Autumn is looking into the archives of the town's history and if there is anything she'll contact me—and I'll get ahold of you. I promise."

Eddie left with his family, and it was tough seeing how dejected he was. I felt guilty that in all the holiday photography excitement I'd forgotten to follow up with Autumn. Before I could forget again, I grabbed my cell and shot off a quick text to my cousin.

She sent a reply almost immediately. It read: *Meet me at the museum tomorrow afternoon. I may have found something.*

"Excellent," I said and slipped my phone back in my pocket. I'd meet up with Autumn tomorrow and see what she'd discovered. Hopefully it would be something that would help Eddie and the other boys gain some closure.

***

At three o'clock on Monday afternoon I knocked on Autumn's office door at the museum. When I heard her voice telling me to come in, I opened the door and discovered that Thomas Drake was sitting with her.

My jaw dropped but I quickly recovered. "Hello, Mr. Drake." I nodded politely.

"Ivy," he said, with a slight smile on his face.

Autumn waved me over to her desk. "It took a little digging but I found some information on the sighting from 1979."

"Oh?" I didn't particularly want to talk about the cryptid in front of Thomas Drake.

He caught my look and smiled. "I dropped by to visit with Autumn—"

"You were checking on me." Autumn rolled her eyes. "You know, I'm not the first person in the world to have twins."

"You're the first person in *my* family to have twins." Thomas said, patting her shoulder. He focused on me. "Autumn mentioned you were looking for some information on sightings of our local version of Bigfoot?"

I crossed my arms over my chest. "Yes."

"I was telling Autumn, that both my father and I were with the group of men who went into the woods in '79 to hunt for the creature."

"You were?" Now he had my attention.

"Yes," he said. "Along with your grandfather."

"I'd like to hear more about that," I said.

Thomas gestured to the remaining chair. "Take a seat and I'll tell you everything I know."

Thomas Drake had been barely twenty-one when he, his father, Silas, my grandpa Morgan, and other men from William's Ford had gone out in search of the creature Steven Waterman had encountered. According to Thomas, they found strange tracks and a bit of long shaggy black fur. They also came across the remains of a deer that had been torn apart. But other than that, they'd found nothing else.

"What about the photographs?" I asked. "Sharon Waterman told me that her father had managed to take a few pictures of the cryptid."

"Yes, I know," he said.

"Well, the photo I saw on the internet looked like it was culled from an old newspaper, and the quality is beyond poor."

Thomas sat back in his chair. "That's because forty years ago we made sure the one clear image of the creature never saw the light of day."

Autumn perked up. "Who's *we*?"

"The members of the magickal council," Thomas said. "Together the council cast a protection spell on the woods, and we took turns keeping watch for several months. The creature never returned, and public interest faded."

"I'm going to take a wild guess that Mr. Waterman was ridiculed for his claims of the encounter," I said.

Thomas grimaced. "It was an unfortunate side effect of our efforts to minimize any attention to the situation. Afterward, his story became a sort of amusing local legend."

I narrowed my eyes. "So we're talking about a magickal cover up?"

"Precisely." Thomas nodded. "If it would have been made public knowledge that a creature was roaming the local woods, the panic it would have caused would have been catastrophic."

"That," Autumn said, "and we're talking the 1970's. The local magickal families and covens were a bit more closeted back then."

"What happened to the photo?" I asked. "Do we know where it is now?"

"We do," Thomas said. "It's in my private library at Drake mansion."

I snapped my head around at his words. "You do realize that there are four teenagers who are going through hell right now because no one believes what happened to them?"

"Yes." His voice was grave. "I've been discreetly checking in on Hunter Roland while he's been recuperating."

"You have been?" Autumn asked.

Thomas nodded. "I also spoke to his doctors. He'll recover, but he's going to need physical therapy."

"How did you manage to speak to his doctors?" I asked

"Being on the hospital's board of directors has its perks." Thomas smoothed back his salt and pepper hair. "A few days ago Duncan mentioned to me that you were researching the attack, and that Autumn was going to check the local history archives, so I came to offer my assistance."

I was slightly mollified by his answer. He sat

there in an expensive suit and overcoat, and literally reeked of sincerity, *and* it was genuine. I knew it to be so because I'd seen him around small children. My nephew Morgan liked him, and Belinda could wrap the man around her pinky finger. Not to mention Thomas was like a father to my cousin Maggie, and filling in like a proud grandpa for her daughter, Willow.

No matter what I'd once thought of him when I was a teenager, the truth was that while Thomas Drake *was* a scary powerful magician, he was also a very kind man. No sooner had the thought crossed my mind—when I suddenly *knew.*

"You're the anonymous donor who started the fund for Hunter," I said.

Thomas brushed at his slacks and said nothing.

"Ten K is a hell of a way to kick start the fundraising," I added.

"That was incredibly generous, Thomas." Autumn said.

"Yes, well..." Thomas smiled a tiny bit. "Let's keep that between us, shall we?"

"I'll protect your anonymity, Mr. Drake." I

smiled. "Besides, I imagine it probably would ruin your bad-ass image if this ever got out."

He inclined his head. "Thank you, Ivy."

"In regards to that old photo you have, I'd really like to see it for myself, and I'd like your permission to share it with Eddie O'Connell. He is one of the most recent people to come in contact with the cryptid."

"Ah, young Mr. O'Connell." Thomas rubbed a hand over his chin.

"Eddie is the second son of Cora O'Connell," Autumn reminded him. "Cora's maiden name was *Lewis*. She's a member of one of the founding magickal families."

Thomas thought it over for a few moments. "Yes, of course. Ronald Lewis. I knew him."

"I'm betting that he was a member of the council back in the 1970's?" I said.

"Yes, and he was a fine magician as well," he said to me. "Autumn tells me that you believe the boy's magick helped save his friends the night of the attack?"

"Yes," I said. "I'm certain that it did."

"How very interesting." Thomas drummed his fingers on his knee. "I believe I'd like to meet young Mr. O'Connell. By all means, bring him with you to the mansion, tonight."

***

Call it luck, or fate, but I had tonight off from the farm. I picked up Eddie at seven o'clock and drove us both to the Drake mansion. He remained silent when I parked the car around back and as we walked across the courtyard. It wasn't until I knocked on the door that he finally spoke.

"I can't believe I'm actually doing this." Eddie shivered in the cold.

"Don't believe everything you've heard about Thomas Drake." I reached over and gave Eddie a bolstering pat on the shoulder. "There's more to him than meets the eye."

"And that's supposed to make me feel better?" Eddie asked.

"I *meant*," I said, "that he's a good man. Don't be nervous."

Eddie scowled at my response, and that frown made me suddenly realize that I hadn't seen him smile the last few times I was with him. Not once. The experience of his friend's attack had changed Eddie O'Connell from a happy-go-lucky-teen, to a serious young man. And that made me sad for him.

My cousin Maggie and her daughter Willow answered the door. "Hey, Ivy!" They both greeted me with smiles and hugs.

I introduced them to Eddie, and Maggie gave him a smile. "Hello again, Eddie."

"Hi, Ms. Parrish." Eddie shuffled his feet and ducked his head.

"Come in, come in!" Maggie didn't miss a beat. She took his arm and steered him inside and out of the cold. "Only four more weeks until your sister's wedding." She held out her hands to take his coat. "Are y'all excited?"

Eddie met her eyes, blushed slightly, and managed to answer. "Uh, yeah. It'll be great."

Oh. I realized. *He might be nervous about seeing Thomas, but he's actually more flustered by Maggie!*

"Hi!" Willow beamed up at Eddie. "I'm Willow."

While Eddie spoke to Willow, I nudged an elbow into my gorgeous cousin's ribs.

Heartbreaker, I thought at Maggie—hard.

She sent me a withering look, and I knew she'd picked up on the telepathic message. Maggie smiled at Eddie and took his offered coat.

I slipped my own coat off and tossed it toward a bench in the foyer. "How goes it, munchkin?" I asked Willow.

"Y'all gotta come see our tree!" Willow said. "It's so big!"

I was hauled off to what the Drakes used as a family room. Willow allowed me enough time to notice the beautifully decorated and lit evergreen garland adorning the main staircase of the house.

Eddie and Maggie fell in step behind us, and I wasn't surprised to discover that the family's main tree was at least ten feet tall. If I had the space for one I'd do the same. It was covered in white and gold ornaments, and many were shaped like golden suns with smiling faces. I spotted moon-shaped decorations as well, with plenty of frosted white and tone-on-tone golden ornaments. A large white and gold bow was being used as a tree topper, and streamers were threaded throughout the branches. It was stunning.

"That's gorgeous," I said to Maggie. "Very winter solstice looking."

Maggie smiled. "Thomas let me decorate the family room this year, so I thought I'd go with an elegant solstice theme. Violet tied up the tree topper for me. I haven't managed to learn how to tie up those big bows."

I nodded. "She always makes it look so easy."

"It's not hard actually," Eddie said. "You just have to train your fingers to hold all the ribbon as you tie the bow."

Maggie smiled. "So says the son and brother of floral designers."

"It's not a big deal." Eddie shrugged.

"Me and Isabel have stockings on the fireplace," Willow announced.

I walked over and inspected them. Two white satin stockings, each embroidered with one of the girl's names, were hung from the mantle. It touched me that the Drakes had included the Vasquez's baby daughter in their family celebrations. Things certainly had changed.

"Well, Santa won't have any trouble finding you," I said to Willow.

"That's what Mama says!" Willows long brown pigtails bounced in her enthusiasm. "I even have a tree in my bedroom, it's all pink!"

"That's very cool." I smiled at her.

"Do you wanna come see my room?" Willow asked us.

Willow," Maggie spoke up. "Ivy and Eddie are here to talk to Thomas."

"Oh," Willow's bottom lip poked out.

"Hey, I'll come up and see it later." I ran my hand over her hair. "And no pouting. Santa's watching."

"Okay," the girl muttered.

"Why don't you walk us to the library?" I said, brightly. "We'll get lost if we try to find the way ourselves."

"I know the way!" Willow said importantly. "Come on!" She grabbed my hand, and Eddie's, towing us along.

Thomas Drake sat behind a massive desk in his personal library. I had been in here a few times and I adored this room. It was loaded with old books, and boasted a gorgeous fireplace that held a crackling fire. The mantle had been decorated for the holidays, and tiny golden lights shone in a lush evergreen swag.

"Uncle Thomas, Ivy and Eddie are here!" Willow announced from the doorway.

Eddie hesitated in the doorway and I gave him a firm push in the back. I stepped into the room behind him. Maggie and Willow slipped away allowing us to speak without being overheard.

Thomas welcomed us and reached out to shake Eddie's hand.

"Thank you for doing this," I began.

Without preamble, Thomas lifted a photo from his desk. "Here is the picture I promised to show you." He held it out. "It needs to stay here, in this house."

I took the photo he held, and my eyes widened at what I saw.

The old photo had been color, but had faded after forty years. It was slightly out of focus and almost a full body shot. The cryptid was huge. Much bigger than I'd thought. I had privately wondered if seeing it through Eddie's memories had distorted my perception of its size somehow, but it hadn't. "No wonder the rangers thought it was a bear." I whistled with appreciation and held out the photo to Eddie.

Eddie took a deep breath, steeling himself before reaching for the photo. He stared at the picture for a moment. "That's the fucker that got Hunter."

Thomas nodded. "Eloquently stated, Mr. O'Connell."

Eddie lifted his eyes to the older man. "Sorry."

"No need," Thomas said. "I share your sentiments."

I pulled the photo down so we could all view it together. "Dark shaggy fur, upright ears and a long tail." I pointed to the features the boys had described.

"Its eyes were bright yellow," Eddie said softly. "I just remembered." He stood staring at the photo with his breathing ragged, and his eyes much too large in his face.

I felt the shiver that ran through him. "Eddie are you all right?"

He nodded. "I'm going to need a second." Eddie shoved the picture at me, turned away, and silently considered the fire.

I addressed Thomas. "Besides the sighting in '79, does the Magickal Council know of any other sightings, or encounters with the cryptid?"

"No," Thomas said. "Not that I know of."

Eddie spun toward Thomas. "So the council knew all this time that the thing was out there...but they *never* warned anyone?"

I started to speak, but Thomas waved me off. "Eddie," he said. "I was only a few years older than you are now when I accompanied my father and the other men from the council on the hunt. We searched off and on for weeks, but never found any definitive sign of the creature." Thomas paused. "I didn't approve of the council's decision to conceal what had happened. But as I said, I was young, and my opinion didn't matter much to the elders."

"Who were the elders that decided to cover all this up?" Eddie asked.

"My father, Silas, Oscar Jacobs, Morgan Bishop..." Thomas ticked the names on his fingers, "Wayne Sutherland, James Proctor, Sven Larson, and your grandfather, Ronald

Lewis."

"Wait," I interrupted. "Did you say Sven *Larson*?"

"Yes." He raised his eyebrows.

My heart started to pound. "Do you know if Sven Larson had a wife named Greta?"

Thomas closed his eyes and thought. "I believe he did. They owned a farm on the outskirts of town. His widow sold the property to her daughter's husband, Ezra McBriar."

"To be clear," I fought to keep my voice calm. "Sven Larson was on the magickal council?"

Thomas nodded. "He was."

Oh my goddess, I thought. *Erik's grandfather had been a magician.* I bit my lip to keep from laughing out loud.

"What does that have to do with anything?" Eddie wanted to know.

"I met Greta Larson this weekend at the farm where I'm taking photographs for the holidays," I explained. "Greta insisted that the vandalism they suffered was because of the Yule lads."

"I'd follow up on that," Thomas said to me.

"Oh, I will." I nodded.

"You said, Ronald Lewis," Eddie reminded Thomas. "Are you telling me that my mom's father was in on the cover up?"

"He was." Thomas' voice was gentle but also serious.

Eddie raked a hand through his hair in frustration. "Do you think my mom knew about any of this?"

"I doubt it," Thomas said.

"What do we do now?" Eddie asked.

"We keep an eye on that park, especially with the Renaissance Faire happening soon," I answered.

"I can't believe they are leaving the park open!" Eddie said, dropping down in a chair. "The Rennies will be camping on Friday and Saturday night. They could be in real danger."

Thomas' brow rose. "Rennies?"

"The Renaissance Faire cast," I explained.

"I wasn't aware they camped overnight," Thomas said.

"Some of the vendors and performers do," I said.

"This *is* problematic," Thomas said.

"Understatement of the year," I quipped.

Eddie sat back in his chair. "What about the tree farm? It runs right along side the park."

"I noticed that Erik McBriar and his father have both been toting firearms out in the fields." I rested my hand on Eddie's arm. "They are taking precautions, but they believe the incident with the cryptid—the dog they lost—was due to coyotes."

"That's better than nothing," Eddie agreed.

"I'll speak to Greta Larson tomorrow," I said. "I'm working until nine, and I'll see if she remembers anything from the incident in 1979."

"Would she even be open to that?" Eddie asked.

I smiled, remembering all the creepy Yuletide legends she'd told me the other day. "I have a hunch that she will."

Before anything else could be said, Willow walked in the room carrying a mug. "I brought hot chocolate for Eddie," she announced.

"Sorry to interrupt," Maggie called from the doorway. "She insisted."

"That's all right." Thomas smiled at the little

girl.

Willow had her tongue between her teeth as she carried the mug in the library. I could see it had sloshed a tad over the sides, but there were still big marshmallows floating on top.

"You need this," Willow said, holding the mug out to Eddie.

"Thanks, Willow." Eddie carefully accepted the sticky mug.

Willow smiled at him. "I put marshmallows in it especially for you."

"Ah sure, okay." Eddie lifted the mug to his lips and sampled. "It's pretty good."

Willow placed her hand on Eddies arm where it rested on the chair. "You were very brave."

Eddie choked on the cocoa. "What?"

Willow leaned in until they were almost nose-to-nose. "You fought a monster," she said quietly. "You saved your friend."

"How did you—" Eddie began.

Willow shrugged. "I just knew."

"I swear," Maggie began, "I never said anything to her."

"Hey, munchkin." I knelt to Willow's level. "Did you feel it in your tummy when you *just knew*?"

"Uh-huh." Willow's unique brown and blue eyes shifted to mine and the expression in them was serious. "I feel it right here," she said, lying her hands over her solar plexus.

"That's how it works for me too." I smiled at the girl.

"So she *is* an intuitive," Thomas said.

Maggie flashed a rueful grin. "Autumn predicted that she was."

Eddie eyeballed the child who stood so seriously before him. "You kinda remind me of Charlie."

"Charlie's my friend." Willow nodded. "She teaches me tricks and stuff."

I couldn't help but snort out a laugh. "Oh, boy."

"Charlie's dad is marrying my sister, Violet," Eddie said to Willow. "In a couple of weeks I'll be Charlie's new uncle."

"Really?" Willow asked with very large eyes.

"Yeah." Eddie tugged on one of Willow's pigtails.

Willow pointed at the mug of cocoa. "You're s'posed to drink it all," Willow said, studying

Eddie.

"Oh, sorry." Eddie started to chug the cocoa, even tipping the mug back to get the marshmallows out of the bottom of the cup. With a dramatic slurp that had Willow giggling, he lowered the mug and swiped at his cocoa mustache.

"Thanks, Willow," he said. "This is the best hot chocolate I've *ever* had."

Willow bounced happily in response, and for a few moments Eddie was actually smiling.

CHAPTER NINE

It was taking longer than I would've liked to find the chance to speak to Greta Larson at the Christmas tree farm. The McBriars had advertised for opportunities for photos on Tuesday and Friday nights, and from open to close on the weekends. Greta only helped on the weekends, and once Friday evening hit, I was told to expect insanity.

According to Diane, the second weekend in December was their biggest period for retail sales. Add to that the local midwinter fair at the park, and it was all hands on deck, so to speak.

I was staging the classic truck for a new batch of holiday photos on Friday afternoon, and was trying something different by rearranging the props. I had stepped back all the way to the end of the tailgate to take a critical look and was considering the composition when I felt a hand at my back.

"Careful."

I discovered that Erik was standing right behind me. "Worried I'll fall off?"

"You were too busy arranging things, I didn't want you to get distracted and step back too far."

He held up a hand, and holding onto the camera around my neck, I took his offered hand with my free one. When our fingers touched, my stomach tightened painfully. Ignoring my reaction, I hopped down.

"Hey, as long as you're here, I wanted to run a request by you," I said, letting go of his hand immediately. "There's a full moon tomorrow night and the forecast is calling for mostly clear skies. So, I was wondering if I could get some photos of the tree fields after close."

"A full moon?" Erik paused over that.

"Yes, a full moon." I resisted the urge to roll my eyes. "It's when the moon appears to be fully illuminated from the earth's perspective. Perhaps you've heard of it?"

He simple gawked at me.

"It happens roughly every twenty-nine days or so..." I added helpfully.

He sent me a withering look. "I know what the full moon is, Ivy."

Ezra and Diane were walking past on their way to the barn, so I hailed them. "Mr. and Mrs. McBriar?"

"Yes?" they asked together.

"I was wondering if it would be all right if I could go out tomorrow evening—once at moonrise and then again after closing—and take some photos of the tree fields and take advantage of the full moon."

"Sure." Ezra smiled. "I bet you'd get some amazing pictures."

"I could use one of the gators," I said, "and drive myself out to the same place I took those engagement photos of Shawna and Brian."

"I'd prefer if you took someone with you." Diane spoke up. "Especially after that animal attack."

"I was very sorry to hear about your old dog," I said.

Diane's smile wobbled. "We've been keeping

the rest of the dogs confined to the retail area, as much as possible."

"Have you seen any other signs of a large predator?" I asked.

"Not recently, but I tell you what, I'll take you to the tree fields tomorrow night." Ezra smiled. "I know right where the moon rises this time of year."

"Thanks," I said. "That will be great!"

"What about the people wanting Christmas pictures?" Erik asked. "We advertised for a photographer to be available—"

"Erik," Diane chided him. "Ivy is not an employee, nor is she on the clock."

"No worries," I said, forcing myself to remain polite. "I'll simply shoot the first set of photos during my dinner break. And the second set will be taken *after* closing."

Ezra gave Erik a look and then addressed me. "Moonrise is around six o'clock. We should probably head out to the field about fifteen minutes beforehand."

"That sounds perfect." I flashed the man a big smile and ignored Erik. "Thank you, Mr. McBriar."

"Of course." Ezra smiled in return. "Now I think we should let our photographer get to work. She has a line starting to form already."

I shot a quick look over my shoulder and saw two families standing at my canopied table. With a wave to Ezra and Diane, I jogged over to the clients.

So much for Erik starting to behave himself, I thought. *The first mention of a full moon and he got all pissy.*

Even as I chatted up the families wanting their pictures taken, I saw Erik out of my peripheral. He was standing a couple of yards away with his arms crossed. Six feet of attitude, staring at me and scowling.

While the first family shuffled over to the truck and the kids climbed in the bed, I lifted my camera and turned. Framing Erik in, I took a few photos of him as he stood there continuing to frown at me.

Oh, and he didn't like that. Not one bit.

"Very sexy!" I called out. "That's right, Erik, give me more of a pout!"

Laughter rang out from the shoppers and staff. Someone let loose a wolf whistle.

"Come on baby, give us a smile!" I called out as the laughter grew louder. "The camera *loves* you!"

A red flush ran up Erik's cheeks. "Very funny," he said. "Let's get back to work, everyone." With a final glare at me, he turned on his heel and walked away.

I lowered the camera and grinned. Doing my best not to giggle at his hasty retreat, I gave my attention back to the young family waiting for their session.

"Okay, guys," I said. "Let's do this."

Erik came stomping back at closing, looking every bit as cranky as he had earlier. I was sitting at the table, adding notes in my laptop about the last set of pictures I'd taken, and concentrating on the task at hand. I had decided after our last encounter that ignoring him would be my best line of defense. Even though I could see him standing a couple of yards away, I refused to acknowledge his presence.

Buck was sitting at my side and the yellow lab's head rested on my lap. Erik called to the dog, and Buck lifted his head. With a canine sigh, the dog dropped his head back on my thigh and ignored Erik as well.

I patted the dog's head. *Good boy,* I thought.

Buck gave a soft *woof* in reply.

I continued to work, even as I heard the gravel crunching beneath his boots as he approached.

Erik stopped right next to my table. "Ivy," he said.

I kept typing, never even sparing him a glance.

"I told Dad, that *I* would take you out to the fields after closing tomorrow," he said. "That way he won't have to do it twice."

"That's not necessary." I hit *save* and closed the laptop. "I can drive myself."

"It *is* necessary."

I stuck my nose in the air. "I beg to differ."

"For safety reasons, it *is* necessary."

"I can take care of myself," I said. "I planned on taking my g—"

"Don't be an ass," he hissed, stepping in closer.

The dog lifted his head and let out a low growl in warning.

Erik stepped back. "Buck just *growled* at

me." He sounded shocked.

"He's picking up on your energy, Erik. You're hostile and he doesn't like it."

"You've turned my own dog against me?" He asked incredulously.

I lifted my eyes and met his. "I'd say your dog has an excellent capacity to judge intentions. You're angry at me and the dog is acting protectively."

Erik held up his hands in surrender. "Look, it's been a long day and I'm sorry for snarling at you, and for earlier. It all came out wrong." He dropped his hands to his sides. "You probably thought I was freaked out about the full moon, but actually I was thinking about all the people who've been coming here to get their pictures taken, by you. Our tree and the gift shop sales are way up this year. That's all because of *you*, and your photography."

I studied him silently for a solid ten seconds. "Did it hurt?" I finally asked.

"What?"

"The apology. I've got money on the table that you rarely, if ever, apologize for anything."

He shifted his stance, and frowned.

"You know," I said sweetly. "If you keep that up you're going to have permanent frown lines on your face. It'll age you by a good ten years."

He gaped at me. "I was *trying* to be nice, Ivy."

"Try harder," I said, completely serious.

He rubbed a hand across his face. "Jesus, you're something."

"So I've been told." I reached for the laptop case and started to put my things away.

"I'm *sorry*," he said, blowing out a long breath. "I never used to have a problem with my temper, but after that fiasco with Raelynn..."

I zipped up the case and stood. "You should let that anger go. You wrap yourself up in it like an armor, which isn't healthy. I bet your stomach bothers you all the time."

Erik blinked. "How the hell did you know that?"

"Intuition. That, and my belly hurts every time you are close and wound up. I can practically feel your stomach lining burning away."

"I thought Holly was the empath."

"My twin and I have more in common than we first thought. I have more of a capacity for empathy and she has more of a talent for—" I cut myself off. There was no point in antagonizing him further. Shutting my mouth, I gathered my things.

"You once said to me that you'd show me what your magickal specialty was."

"I said, I'd show you *if* I thought you could handle it." I slung the strap for the camera case over my shoulder. "Your current behavior shows me that you can't."

"Try me," he said.

I sighed and debated with myself over what I was about to do. For the past year, I'd adopted a sort of mantra. *A wise practitioner avoids public or unnecessary displays of power,* I reminded myself. By sticking to that, I'd managed to avoid problems and drama. I wasn't a kid anymore. I had a career to build and a professional reputation to establish.

"Perhaps, something small," I finally said.

Erik folded his arms. "Go ahead."

I checked over my shoulder to ensure that we were alone. Once I saw that we were, I focused on the ink pen I'd left lying on the table and sent it up to hover in the air directly in front of Erik's face.

He flinched back so hard that he almost fell over one of my chairs.

I raised an eyebrow. "You *did* ask."

His eyes were huge. "How did you do that?"

"Magick," I said simply. "My specialty is PK, what is known as psychokinesis. They used to refer to it as telekinesis." I concentrated and sent the pen spinning slowly, end over end while he stared at it slack-jawed.

"Jesus!" His breathing was ragged and he quickly dropped in the chair.

Aw, hell, I thought. *His knees gave out on him.* "I didn't mean to frighten you," I said softly.

He rubbed a hand over his face. "You surprised me, but you didn't scare me." He looked from the spinning pen and back to me. "This is amazing. Can Holly do this kind of thing as well?"

I didn't answer that question. Instead, I held up my hand and the pen zipped straight through the air and right into my fingers. "And this concludes our demonstration for the day."

"Wow!" Erik shook his head in amazement. "I guess you showed me."

"You asked," I reminded him, again.

His lips quirked up in a half smile. "That'll teach me to be careful with what I say to you, from now on." He began to laugh, but it wasn't directed *at* me. He was mostly laughing at himself.

I narrowed my eyes at the unexpected change in his attitude. "Look on the bright side, Erik. I'm only going to be here for a few more weeks. Then you won't have to see me anymore."

"I don't mind you being here," Erik said, gruffly.

I rolled my eyes. "Well, aren't you a charmer?"

He gave me a slow look. "I can be."

I snorted at that. "Yes, suaveness and good manners practically radiate from you, McBriar. Not unlike denim and flannel."

He grinned at my snark and picked up the tripod and my large prop bag. "I'll help you carry all this to your car."

"That's not necessary," I began.

He stood. "Since I don't imagine you're going to make it go floating through the air—"

"I would never purposefully draw attention like that to myself in public!" I hissed.

"I was trying to make a joke."

I frowned. "I'm not laughing."

"I've been rude to you twice today." He rested his hand cautiously on my arm. "At least let me try and make up for it."

"Relax, Erik." I patted his hand where it rested on my elbow. "I won't turn you into a frog. Besides, I don't want to put you to any trouble."

"You're not," he said.

I shrugged. "Suit yourself." Easing away from him, I gave the dog a pat on the head, grabbed the camera and laptop cases, and headed for the employee parking lot.

Erik and the dog both followed me out to my car. I loaded everything in the back and let the trunk slam closed, but I hadn't realized he'd been standing so close, and accidentally bumped into him. "Oops. Sorry." I immediately pulled back.

He steadied me by putting his hands on my arms. "If I've made you feel uncomfortable, then I truly am sorry, Ivy."

I hadn't *been* uncomfortable, at least not until this moment. Because standing in his arms in that dark parking lot was making me feel slightly ill at ease.

Not because I was afraid, but because something had changed between the two of us. The waxing moon shone overhead, and the frosty stars were twinkling. As I gazed into his bright blue eyes; my heart gave a little hitch—and *that* surprised me.

Spooked, I stepped back out of his arms. "See you tomorrow." I was astounded at how difficult it was to make my words sound casual.

He stayed where he was, watching me. "Yes, you will."

I took another cautious step back. "Good night."

He nodded. "See you."

***

I gave myself a very firm lecture as I drove

to the farm on Saturday morning. Erik McBriar might be ruggedly handsome, but he was *not* my type. Yes, he had that whole broad shouldered, blue-eyed, blonde thing going for him. But he was also prejudiced about Witches. Besides, he was a Protestant whereas I followed the old religion. I preferred to date men of a like mind, or at least those who were open-minded. I had never been into mundane farm boys, before.

I was, I assured myself, typically attracted to more of the 'dark poet' sort of man.

Of course my last serious relationship had involved a scholarly and serious, hereditary male magician who'd come from a long line of Witches. However, Nathan Pogue and I hadn't been end game. I'd known it and so had he. Which was probably why we'd somehow managed to remain friends after he'd gone back to Massachusetts and I'd stayed here...

Wait, where was I?

Oh yeah. A mundane, rugged farm boy could *never* be the love of my life. The idea was laughable.

I eased my car down the gravel lane to the

farm. Even in the morning there was a good amount of traffic. I pulled around behind *Mistletoe Mercantile*, parked, and mentally prepared myself for another day of holiday photos.

The day was busy with plenty of customers wanting mini sessions. At a quarter to six, I took my dinner break and went to my car to stow my laptop. Since no one was around in the employee parking area, I was able to discreetly slip my waist holster on under my insulated vest. Considering the night photo shoot, and our close proximity to the animal attacks, it was a wise precaution.

I knew that both Erik and his father had remained armed since the animal attack in late November. There were also rifles discreetly stowed in all the pickup trucks the employees drove when they hauled out the customers to the cutting fields. But my gut told me to be extra careful tonight. Maybe it was the full moon enhancing my intuition. Perhaps it was something else. Either way, I wasn't taking any chances.

Once I had the holster situated, I walked to

the front of the gift shop in time for Ezra McBriar to arrive in a pickup. I quickly hopped in with my camera around my neck and my tripod in hand. Ezra went around the back way, avoiding the trucks that hauled customers out to the cutting fields, and far away from the folks cutting their own trees. We zipped along, heading towards the newer fields where the evergreen trees were still growing.

Fortunately for me, Ezra did know exactly where the moon would be rising. I was able to set up in moments. I'd had plenty of practice photographing that series of eclipses a few years prior, so I knew what to expect for exposure and light settings. Making minute modifications for the light, I shot dozens of photos while the moon rose, pale yellow above the horizon.

I ignored my cold nose, fingers and toes, and focused on the moon, the rolling fields of trees, and the forest in the background. When my timer sounded, I broke everything down and started back to the truck where Ezra had waited.

It was a very still night, and my boots made crunching noises on the frozen ground. Now that I wasn't photographing the scenery, it was creepy out in this distant part of the fields. Surprised at my reaction, I shuddered from a combination of cold and the atmosphere. The hair on the nape of my neck prickled and I swung around, checking behind me.

I held my breath and waited, convinced I had seen someone walking through the trees and off to my left. For a moment I thought it was Ezra, but he was sitting patiently in the truck with the window open. I waited a moment longer, but nothing seemed to be moving, so I quickened my pace and hurried back to him.

"Ready to head back?" Ezra asked, all good cheer.

"You betcha!" I smiled and tugged my gloves back on, hoping to warm up my chilled fingers.

By time the farm closed at nine pm, I was more than happy to step inside the gift shop and warm up with some of Grandma Larson's hot cocoa.

"You be careful out there under that moon tonight, *musling*," she warned me.

"Moose-ling?" I chuckled over the word and added another marshmallow to my mug.

"Little mouse," she translated.

"I am always careful," I tossed her a wink. "I've taken precautions."

She leaned closer to me. "I didn't mean the gun. There are creatures out and about. The wild hunt, it roams on nights like these."

Her words caused my solar plexus to go tight. It was then that I realized that Greta *saw* a great deal. More so than anyone else was even aware of. "Grandma Larson," I began, "what do you remember about the sighting of a creature in the woods back in the winter of 1979?"

"Heard about that, did you?"

"Thomas Drake told me recently that your husband Sven was part of the *council* of men who went out to investigate."

She nodded. "He was and he did."

I glanced carefully around, making sure that no one else was close enough to overhear our conversation. "Did your husband know, or have any theories as to what the creature actually was?"

"I know that he discussed the matter with your grandfather," she said after a few humming seconds of silence.

"And?"

"My Sven thought it was possible that whatever Mr. Waterman had seen, it might have been a creature from the *vilde jat*—wild hunt."

"And the wild hunt rules during the darkest days before Yule." I remembered.

"The Allfather, he will protect us." Greta nodded. "After our dog was attacked, and then the Yule lads brought their mischief, I made offerings to him and there have been no more problems."

"Is the farm—your original property—warded?" I asked.

"It was many years ago, before Sven passed."

"Have you strengthened the boundaries lately, yourself?"

Grandma Larson shook her head. "He was the mage, not I."

I sipped my cocoa and thought it over. "You said you made offerings to the Allfather?"

"*Ja*," she nodded. "I did."

"Smart." I nodded in agreement.

"As my Sven would have done."

"What did you do, exactly?" I smiled at the

gleam in her eye.

"A bit of this and that. Odin is the god of my ancestors," she whispered. "I honor him in my own way."

"Did you use the valknut?" I asked, thinking of the old Norse symbol of three interlocking triangles.

"I drew it and other runes close to the farm stand, and in the shop where they wouldn't be seen. I tucked tiny pieces of mistletoe in the corners of the shop too."

"Kept it low-key, did you?" I grinned. "That sounds perfect to me. I've been carrying mistletoe for the past few weeks." I pulled out the fabric sachet bag from my coat pocket and showed it to her.

"Did you gather that from our apple tree?"

"No." I shook my head. "This was taken from the local woods, where the attack on the boys happened."

Grandma Larson's eyes narrowed. "Is that right?"

"We found this in the exact spot where the cryptid let go of Hunter Roland. I figure a combination of the mistletoe and my friend

Eddie's magick may have stopped things from getting any worse."

"This Eddie, who is his family?" She asked.

"Eddie is the grandson of Ronald Lewis."

"I remember that name," she said. "He had a daughter, Cora. Her married name is O'Connell."

"That's right," I said.

Diane was behind the front counter, and she looked over at her mother and I standing together. I smiled and waved casually.

Grandma Larson sighed. "Diane, she never knew about her father. He taught her the tales of the Norse gods when she was small, but my daughter, she has forgotten them."

"I understand." I met her gaze and held it. "You can trust me. I won't betray your confidence."

"Take this." Grandma Larson pressed a wooden disk in my hand. "It belonged to my Sven, it may offer you some protection."

I saw a slim circle of wood, slightly larger than a silver dollar. The disk was old, had been shellacked, and in the center the valknut had been wood burnt.

I tried to hand it back. "You should keep this with you for your own protection."

She refused it. "I have other things, *min lille heks*."

"What does that Danish phrase mean?" I asked with a smile.

Grandma Larson was about to answer, when Erik walked into the shop. He saw us standing together and headed toward us.

"*Min lille heks,* means," she whispered in my ear, "my little Witch."

With a smile I tucked the talisman in my back pocket. "Thank you, Grandma Larson."

She patted my shoulder. "Of course."

"What are you two whispering about?" Erik asked.

"My cocoa recipe," his grandmother lied smoothly. "I was telling Ivy that it's a family secret."

Family secrets, I thought and fought not to laugh. Erik's grandfather had been on the magickal council. His grandmother was secretly Pagan.

And he had absolutely no idea.

CHAPTER TEN

For the second round of pictures, we returned to the same spot Ezra had brought me to earlier. However, clouds were beginning to move in, and the temperatures had dipped below freezing. I quickly set up the tripod, pulled my cap further over my ears, and got down to business taking photos. Erik leaned against the tailgate of the farm truck with his arms crossed over his chest, silently watching me.

Since it was more of a curious sort of observation, as opposed to suspicious, it didn't bother me much.

I'd been working for about ten minutes before he broke the silence. "Will it disturb your work if I ask you something?"

I repositioned the camera and waited for the

clouds to slide past the moon. "Go ahead."

"You seem like you've been enjoying yourself while you've been here at the farm."

"I have."

"I didn't expect that you would," Erik said. "Be comfortable, on the farm, that is."

I spared him a look. "McBriar, my father lives on a farm in Iowa. I spent most my summers and every other winter break there, when I grew up."

Erik shifted his stance. "Really?"

"Yes," I said. "I know exactly how hard farmers work."

He stuck his hands in his coat pockets. "I'm trying to picture you driving a tractor."

"Be assured that I can." I stuck my nose in the air. "My father taught me how to shoot and how to hunt too."

"What did you hunt?"

"Deer and pheasant." I blew on my bare fingers to warm them up. "Sometimes duck."

"What guns do you use to hunt with?" he asked.

"For duck and pheasant I used a 20 gauge shotgun. For deer hunting, a .30-30. I also own a .380 handgun."

"Well, holy shit," Erik laughed. "I would have never expected that."

"Why?" I asked, crossly. "Because I'm female?"

He wiped the smile off his face. "No, of course not. I'm surprised, because it didn't fit with what I already knew about you."

"Sweetie, what you *know* about me wouldn't fit in your back pocket."

Erik pushed away from the bed of the truck and walked over. "I think I'm starting to get that."

"I hope you didn't strain yourself too hard while working it all out."

He snorted out a laugh, and I worked hard to keep a haughty expression on my face. Now that he was standing right next to me and smiling, my stomach twisted. I didn't like that he was being so easygoing and friendly. "Out of my way, Erik. I have work to do."

"Why are you acting so nervous all of the sudden?" he asked, even as he moved a tad closer.

I jerked a shoulder. "I'm not nervous. I'm

annoyed, because you are in my way." I twisted my head to look up at him, fully intending to put him in his place with a snippy comment. But when my eyes met his, every sassy word I'd intended froze in my throat.

Our eyes locked and we stood under that full moon, in the cold, completely alone. The sharp scent of pine surrounded us, and when he reached for my hands, I jumped.

"Your hands are cold," he said. "You should put your gloves back on."

"It's hard to operate the camera wearing winter gloves..." I began and my words stumbled to a halt when he gently rubbed my cold fingers with his hands.

"What are you doing?" I asked suspiciously.

"Warming up your hands." He lifted my fingers to his mouth and blew on them, and my heart slammed into my ribs. "You're trembling, Ivy," he pointed out.

"I'm cold," I corrected, as my heart began to speed up. "It's cold out here."

"Let's fix that then," he said and pulled me a bit closer.

I knew the kiss was coming, and I didn't play

coy. Because I was kind of curious. *Curious, and that was all*, I told myself, even as I rose to my toes to meet him halfway.

Our lips met and it was warm and soft. The kiss held for a few moments, before he pulled back, searching my face for my reaction. He'd given me only the barest of tastes, and I found that I wanted more. Much more.

Which was stupid. *Stupid,* I reminded myself.

Nose to nose with him I fell back on my best defense: snark. "Did all this outdoorsy talk about hunting and rifles turn you on, McBriar?"

"No." His voice was low. "It was all you." He pulled me a bit closer, staring down into my eyes for a few seconds, and waited. It seemed like forever until he slowly lowered his head and kissed me again.

I let my head fall back, inviting him to take the kiss deeper. When his tongue slid over mine, I groaned and pulled him even more snugly against me.

His hands moved up from my back to sink into my hair. I felt my sock cap get knocked off my head and our kiss went on and on. I'm not sure how long we would have stood there kissing each other under that full moon, but I was distracted by the oddest sensation in my back pocket.

Something was heating up and it was killing the moment for me...then I remembered. *The valknut talisman was in my pocket*. There was the loud snap of a branch, and we broke apart, simultaneously turning in the direction of the noise.

I stood, still in Erik's arms, and narrowed my eyes at the movement about twenty yards to our right. Something was moving slowly through the young trees. It was dark enough that I couldn't make it out clearly, but it was big enough that I truly didn't want to.

"What is that?" Erik's voice was a mere breath of a sound.

The clouds shifted and moonlight illuminated the field. What I saw had my jaw dropping and my heart slamming against my ribs. It was the cryptid.

"Get to the truck," Erik whispered.

"I'm not leaving my camera."

"I'm not leaving *you*, and the rifle is in the

case, in the bed of the truck."

"I'm armed," I said, reaching for my holster.

"Thank god," he breathed. "I'll get your camera for you."

"It's attached to the tripod," I whispered.

"I'll grab the whole thing."

I nodded, and as quietly as possible we moved apart. I'd listened very carefully to the descriptions from the boys. I'd viewed the old photo, even seen it through Eddie's memories. But nothing came close to seeing the creature first-hand.

I drew the gun, clicked off the safety and tracked the movement of the cryptid. Good news? It wasn't moving any faster. Bad news? It was still coming closer. Erik picked up the tripod and camera with one hand and rested his other on my back. As one, we backed toward the truck.

"Jesus," Erik breathed, "those eyes. That's *not* a bear."

The wind shifted and we got a whiff of the creature. I tried not to gag. The boys were right, it did stink.

The half dozen backward steps we took to

the truck were some of the longest of my life. I felt my back come to rest against Erik's shoulder as he opened the truck door and shoved the equipment across the bench seat. But before I could even begin to climb inside the truck, the cryptid growled and began to rush forward.

I sighted down the barrel and fired once, then twice, and it seemed to falter. Two seconds later and it was moving again straight for us. I shot for a third time, and it stopped.

"Move!" Erik yelled. He put a hand on top of my head and shoved me straight into the cab. I pointed the gun to the floor and slid across the seat with him right behind me. The door slammed shut and I spun to kneel on the seat, to look out the rear window. Terrified, that the cryptid would hurl itself against the back of the truck.

Erik turned the key in the ignition, and the field before us was instantly flooded with light. However, the area behind us where the creature had been was still fairly dark. He slapped the truck in drive, I had barely enough time to grab ahold of the back of the bench seat before the truck lurched forward.

"I don't see anything behind us," I said as we took off over the tree field.

We hit a bump and my head bounced lightly against the roof of the cab. "Ivy, sit down!" he ordered.

"Yeah," I agreed, and dropped back down to my butt and felt that wooden disc in my pocket. *Thank you Grandma Larson,* I thought. *You probably saved our lives*. I stared out the windshield and shivered.

"You hit it, didn't you?" Erik asked.

"I think so," I said, putting the safety back on. "The second shot for sure."

"What the hell was that?" Erik asked.

"The cryptid."

"The *what*?" His voice went up.

"Cryptid, is the term used for an undocumented creature—"

"Like Bigfoot or something?"

"Sort of." I pushed my camera and tripod down to the floorboards with one hand, so they wouldn't bounce around. I kept the gun gripped tightly in my other. There was no way I was letting go of it. "A cryptid is an animal from folklore. Think mythological."

"Are we talking about a monster?" Erik demanded as he continued to drive. "Something supernatural?"

"Maybe," I said. "But I'm sure that was the same creature that attacked the boys in the park." I nervously checked the rearview mirror. "I don't see it behind us."

Erik swung the truck to a gravel road and punched the accelerator. "Unless it can run faster than the truck, you probably won't."

I blew out a long shaky breath as we sped back toward the farm.

"You handled yourself well out there," Erik said after a moment.

"Thank you." My hands were shaking, but he didn't need to know that.

"You've got balls, Ivy. You're a damn good shot, and I can't think of another woman who would calmly hold her ground against a large animal attack."

"Remind me to introduce you to my sister-in-law," I said.

Erik shook his head. "I'm just thankful we're safe."

"Me too."

He dropped a hand on my thigh. "And that's because of you."

I wasn't sure how to respond to his compliment. Before I could work out what to say, he pulled his cell phone from his coat pocket. "Call Dad," he said into the phone, and the phone automatically dialed.

While Erik alerted his father, I checked over my shoulder again. I saw nothing but the moonlight over the tree fields. The creature didn't seem to be following us, and as we hurried back to the farm stand, I knew the night was about to get a whole lot crazier.

***

I'd gone home well after midnight. The police were called and after they had arrived, they'd taken my statement. The general consensus was that either there was a bear on the property or there was someone dressed up and trying to frighten folks. That last scenario concerned me more than a little. After their initial search of the fields, and after the police confirmed that my gun was indeed registered to me, they'd told me I could go.

I spent the rest of the night unable to sleep and staring at my ceiling. I kept replaying everything over and over in my mind. I couldn't believe I'd shot at the cryptid, and was relieved that we had managed to escape unharmed. I tried not to dwell on what *could* have happened, but the adrenalin had yet to fade.

Back and forth my mind went, and sleep eluded me. I don't know which was a bigger shock to my system, the cryptid, or the fact that I'd been making out with Erik McBriar under a full moon.

And holy shit, when we had kissed, *nothing* else had mattered. It was a damn good thing that talisman Grandma Larson had given me had done its job, otherwise we'd have been monster chow.

Eventually it was morning. I staggered out of bed and threw myself in the shower. I was scheduled to be back at the tree stand taking holiday photos by 11:00 am.

The temperature was currently in the high 20's, and snow was predicted for tonight with the snow starting somewhere after 4:00 pm, and the expected amounts were vague. Anywhere from one inch to six inches was possible. I sat at my desk in my robe, with the news playing in the background, and cleaned the handgun very thoroughly. Staying busy kept my mind from dwelling on Erik.

Lexie poked her head in, “Hey, Ivy.”

“Morning, Lexie.”

“I wanted to talk to you before you left for the day.” She came over and sat on the couch.

I yawned. “Guess you heard about the excitement at the farm last night?”

“I’d prefer to hear your side of it.”

“Okay,” I said, and filled her in, mostly. I only told Lexie that I’d been out with Erik taking photographs of the full moon over the fields. I didn’t mention the make out session to my sister-in-law, that was private. Besides, she’d tease me unmercifully if she knew.

“I’m so glad you had your .038 with you last night,” Lexie said, as I secured the handgun back in my gun safe. “Otherwise, who knows what would have happened out there.”

I locked the safe. “It was scary.” I could say

that to Lexie, she was one of the few people who would really understand. "I didn't sleep much last night. I kept replaying the whole thing over in my mind."

Lexie got up and gave me a hug. "All that practice at the range, paid off."

"Yes it did." I hugged her back. "I think I'll play it safe, stay put, and take photographs by the gift shop today."

Lexie frowned over at the weather segment on the news. "Better bundle up and wear your snow boots."

While the chipper weatherman rambled on about the storm front, I scowled and wondered how in the hell the guy could get away with such an ambiguous description of the approaching winter storm.

With the weather in mind, I layered up with long-sleeved thermal underwear and slipped my jeans and a black bulky sweater over that. I did my face and went with a dark smoky eye and deep burgundy lipstick. Yes, the cosmetics were the most dramatic I'd worn since starting the gig at the tree farm. But after everything that had happened, the moment with Erik, and the cryptid, I'd take all the empowerment or protection that I could get.

I dug through my jewelry box and found a pair of silver earrings shaped like crescent moons. I added my family crest pendant and felt a tad more like myself.

I pulled on two layers of socks, my snow boots, and got out my heaviest winter coat. Finally I added a burgundy scarf, knit hat, and grabbed my camera and laptop cases. I checked my reflection in the mirror before I left. The heavier cosmetics, thigh length black coat, and more gothic clothing were like armor, I decided.

"Speaking of..." I mumbled and backtracked to my nightstand. Grabbing the talisman from Greta Larson, I slipped it in my coat pocket.

Once I arrived at the farm, it was Grandma Larson who took me aside and informed me that the area where we'd spotted the cryptid had been searched by both the police and the conservation department again this morning. Unfortunately, there were no prints—the ground was too frozen for there to have been any. Neither was there any scat, or fur left behind. They had located my hat that I'd forgotten about, *and* the bullet casings from the rounds I'd fired.

However, with no concrete signs of a human trespasser, or a large predator, there was nothing they could do.

I listened to Erik's grandmother, and afterward thanked her for the talisman. When I explained how it had warned me of danger, she smiled and said that she was happy Odin was watching over me.

I'm not sure if it was Odin or what god had smiled down upon me, but I was thankful nonetheless. Erik was busy today running the farm, and I didn't see him at all. I knew he was out there working because I heard his voice over the walkie-talkie all day. But he never came to see me.

It surprised me that *I* needed to see him. I wasn't even sure why. I was hardly the type of person to need a man to tell me things were going to be all right. I could take care of myself, and anyone else, if needs be. Hadn't I proven that last night?

But still, I missed him. I casually asked one

of the staff where he was, and was informed that his folks had gone to town to visit his sister and her family, apparently one of the older kids had a recital or something. Which meant Erik was managing the farm on his own today.

Perhaps him being so busy today was for the best, because I had no idea how I'd react to seeing him after everything that had happened. I didn't regret the kiss. It did, however, make things a tad awkward going forward.

Maybe he was avoiding me? Maybe he regretted the kiss? Those thoughts had my stomach dropping. I mean, it wasn't like we had a chance to even enjoy it, as we were basically running for our lives because of the cryptid.

Silently, I corrected myself. We hadn't run for our lives. I'd stood my ground, fired at it, and when it faltered, stumbled...whatever, we'd gotten the hell out of there. Which was realistically the smartest move. Hadn't Ezra said that repeatedly last night? Hadn't Lexie said the same this morning?

Erik hadn't even walked me to my car when I'd left last night. Then again the cops had been everywhere, and he had been kind of busy speaking to his father and the police…With a growl of frustration, I yanked my hat down further over my ears.

This was stupid. Standing there mooning over a man and obsessing over a kiss.

Deliberately I shut my eyes, grounded and centered my energy, and told myself to focus on the job at hand. When a couple approached my photography booth, I jumped to my feet and greeted them with a big smile.

"Hello!" I said cheerfully. "Are you interested in having a mini holiday photo session today?"

By late afternoon, I had managed to get three photo sessions in. The tree farm wasn't as busy today, and I was sure that was because of the impending weather. My phone had been sending me alerts and the predicted snow totals had only increased as the day progressed. Now they were calling for eight to ten inches of snow to fall.

You could smell the predicted snow in the air, and as it finally began to fall late in the afternoon, the customers dwindled off to zero.

Grandma Larson sent all the gift shop

employees home before the roads got too bad, and I stayed to give her a hand with running the closing reports and shutting down the retail space. After last night I didn't want her to be alone, and goddess knows I had plenty of experience with retail after working in my family's store for so many years.

I peeked out the shop's window and saw that the snow was falling thick and fast. While it was magickal and amazing seeing the snow come down that hard, I still didn't want her driving home in it. So I shooed her along, promising to lock up and head home myself. I almost bust a gut laughing when she hopped in an old muscle truck and took off towards her farmhouse on the far western side of the property.

I waited, watching until I saw her pull into her driveway at the top of the far hill. She flashed the porch light at me, and I raised my hand in a wave, acknowledging that she was inside. I slipped back in the retail space and was starting to count down the drawer for her when the walkie-talkie crackled to life behind me.

"Grandma, it's Erik. You should lock up,

leave things as they are and head up to your house. The roads are going to get bad, fast. I don't want you driving in this."

I grabbed the walkie-talkie and pushed the button to speak. "Hey Erik," I did my best to sound nonchalant. "It's Ivy. I sent your grandma home already and I'm—"

"Ivy?" he interrupted. "What in the hell are you still doing here?"

"I told you, I sent your grandmother home and I'm closing up for her."

"Where are you right now?" Erik demanded.

I rolled my eyes at the walkie-talkie. "In the gift shop counting down the drawer—"

"Damn it!"

"—And, you're welcome," I said dryly.

"I thought everyone had already gone home. Stay put." His voice sounded angry. "I'm on my way to the gate. Give me fifteen minutes."

I set the walkie-talkie back in its cradle to recharge. "To think I spent most of my day fretting over that kiss." I grumbled. "And he's all barking orders and telling me what to do. That shit is hardly charming behavior."

Feeling pissy, I quickly finished counting

down the drawer. I slipped the cash into the deposit bag, cut the lights, and gathered up my equipment bags. After re-buttoning my coat, I headed out the back toward the employee parking area.

I'd taken about five steps when I realized how very serious the winter storm was. I squinted up at the dark sky and rewrapped my scarf. "Wow, it's really coming down." I slogged through the snow to my car with the intention of warming it up so I could drive home, Erik's orders be damned. I was reaching for the door when a flash of lightning was immediately followed by a crack of thunder, and I jumped. Hard.

"Holy shit," I said, awed. "It's thunder snow."

One of the farm trucks came slowly around the side of the shop. The headlights from the truck illuminated how huge the snowflakes were. The driver's side window came down and Erik leaned out. "I told you to wait."

I glared at him. "Well, I decided to ignore your *charming* instructions, McBriar."

"You won't make it home in your car," Erik

said. "Not in a storm like this."

Another crack of thunder punctuated his words, and I stood in that dumping snow and glared at him for a solid ten seconds. "Damn it," I muttered. With a sigh, I walked toward his truck, hauling all my equipment.

"Do you want a hand?" Erik asked.

"No. I've got it."

"Get in," Erik said and hit the button for the door locks.

I walked around the front of his truck, swung my stuff inside the cab, and climbed in. "Thanks for giving me a ride home," I said, after shutting the door.

The look he gave me was incredulous. "I'm not taking you home. I'm not driving anywhere in this. You're going to have to stay at the farmhouse tonight."

I paused in the act of brushing snow from my hair. "Excuse me?"

"Relax, Ivy. You can sleep in one of the guestrooms or something." He put the truck in gear and slowly drove out of the lot.

Guestroom, I thought. *Perfect. I'd stick to his parents like glue, be cheerful and get through an evening with Prince Charming. No Biggie. His folks would be the perfect buffer.* "That's very kind of your parents to put me up for the night."

"My folks had nothing to do with it," Erik said. "They aren't even at home. Dad called me a bit ago and said they were staying the night with Ginny and her family. They don't want to risk the roads in the storm."

Figures, I thought sourly. "So we'll be alone."

"Just us and the dog," Erik said. "I promise to be a gentleman, you'll be perfectly safe."

I snorted with laughter. "Set your ego aside, McBriar. I'm not afraid to be alone with you."

One side of his mouth kicked up in a smile. "I never thought you would be."

CHAPTER ELEVEN

Well, so much for my amazing intuition, I thought to myself. *I sure as hell didn't see this one coming.* I sat silently in the cab of the truck as Erik drove across the farm. We traveled past the wedding barn, to the far eastern side of the property. I'd been so busy telling myself not to dwell on the close call with the cryptid, *or* to even think about that kiss all day long, that I'd shut myself off from my psychic abilities. Landing myself in this uncomfortable situation.

I snuck a peek over at Erik as he navigated the snowy farm roads. I wasn't sure if I found it annoying or reassuring that he didn't seem the least bit nervous or uncomfortable about the entire 'spend the night' situation.

I shifted my attention back to the road and

saw the McBriar farmhouse waiting on the crest of a hill. A wind break had been created with trees, and the house was surrounded on three sides by evergreens. Colored lights and pine roping hung in swags from the front porch, and with the heavy snow it all resembled a holiday painting.

As we drove closer I could see other deciduous trees had been planted in the yard. The farmhouse was a classic two story with a wide covered front porch. It was pretty and welcoming. Erik drove around to the side, parked the truck and hopped out. I climbed out the opposite side, grabbed my gear, and followed him through the rapidly increasing snow on the ground to the porch.

He unlocked the door, pushed it open, and Buck shot out. The dog dove headfirst into the snow with a joyous bark. I started to laugh as Buck pranced around, biting at the snow on the ground and snapping at random snowflakes that fell from the sky. The yellow lab took off at a sprint and ran back and forth across the front yard, with as much energy as a puppy.

Erik shook his head. "Go. Get it out of your

system," he said to the dog, laughing at his antics. He held the door open for me. "Come in, Ivy."

"Thank you." I nodded and stepped inside. I looked around at the interior of the house and found an old wooden bench, plump with pillows in red and white against the wall in the entry way. A heavy white shelf with old metal hooks hung above it, and a rustic old farm sign rested on the shelf. I unwrapped my scarf and hung it on a hook.

He shut the door behind us and began to unzip his heavy work coat. "You should probably call your family, and let them know that you won't be driving home in the storm," he suggested.

"I will." Beyond the entryway I saw that the McBriars' living room space was cleverly decorated. Done in a rustic farmhouse theme, there were warm white walls, a beige sectional, and holiday pillows in white, red and black were scattered across it. There was a big wooden sled being used as a coffee table, and I spotted other sturdy antiques around the room. A tall, live tree was lit in the corner. The room was like a magazine spread for country decorating, and I itched to photograph simply *everything*.

"Must be nice to have family in the antiquing business," I said, admiring the way the room had been decorated.

Erik pulled off his boots and set them to the side. "It's home. I'll get a fire started." He moved to the brick fireplace and began to set kindling in place.

I hung up my coat and placed my camera bag and prop bag on the bench in the entry. I tugged off my boots as well and placed them next to Erik's. Once that was done, I padded across the living room in my socks.

After sitting on the couch, I shot off a group text to the family. Lexie called me back immediately.

I hit 'accept' on the screen. "Hello?"

"I was about to call you." Lexie's voice came through loud and clear. "I'm glad you're staying put. We're encouraging folks not to travel unless it's an emergency."

"I'm staying at the McBriars' house tonight, so no worries."

"Good, one less person for me to rescue."

"Be safe, Lexie," I said before ending the call.

"Is your sister-in-law working tonight?" Erik asked.

"Apparently." I slipped my phone back in my hip pocket. *How polite we were to each other,* I thought.

"I'm hungry," Erik said. "How do you feel about sandwiches?"

"Sounds good to me." I stood. "Let me give you a hand."

He smiled. "I'll call the dog in and we can get started."

Buck was wound up when he came back inside. Erik wisely opened a door from the mud room off the kitchen to call the dog in. He tried to snag him and dry him off with a big towel, but the dog shook snow all over the mud room floor.

"Buck!" I called the lab's name. "Sit." With a whine the dog plopped his rump on the tile floor. I took the towel from Erik. "Now, behave yourself," I told the dog.

Erik grinned as I dried off the dog. "You're

going to have to teach me how you do that. He never minds me as well as he listens to you."

"It's one of my many gifts," I said airily, and that made him chuckle.

Once the dog had been dealt with, we washed our hands and Erik put together a couple of sandwiches. He was surprisingly easy to be around, and there was no awkwardness between us. I'd held my breath for the first half hour or so, wondering if he would try and kiss me again, but he never made a romantic move.

It was probably wishful thinking on my part. Because even though he was driving me crazy imagining what could have been between us, the truth was there were no sidelong glances, no lingering touches, and no sexy overtones. I guessed he had decided to shrug off the whole kiss under the full moon. Which was probably for the best.

We were too different to work out as a couple.

Buck lay under the kitchen table and Erik and I ate our sandwiches, like old friends. I was silently congratulating myself on how well the evening had been going thus far, when the power went out.

"Well, shit," he said.

"Good thing you have a fireplace," I said, and pulled my phone from my pocket. I held it up like a flashlight. "Got any candles around here?"

"Mom has some decorative ones sitting on the mantle," Erik said, standing up.

I stood as well. "Well, I'd start with those."

I helped Erik locate and light the tapers on the mantle, and then he rooted around for a few more candles and emergency flashlights. He called and checked on his grandmother. She assured him that she was fine, and had plenty of firewood. We had firewood too, but Erik informed me that most of it was stacked out back.

Which was how I found myself sitting on the hearth with Buck for company, and waiting while Erik went out to bring in more firewood to keep the living room warm.

I heard the back door open and rose to my feet. Going directly to the mudroom, I discovered that Erik had loaded up a wheelbarrow full of logs, and had pushed it up on the porch and close to the doorway. I started grabbing logs from him and stacking them on the tile floor as he passed them to me. Between the two of us it only took a couple of minutes.

"I'll be back." He smiled, pulled his hood up farther over his head and went back out.

Buck stood by my side, whining. "It's okay," I told the dog. "He'll be back in a couple minutes."

But a few minutes stretched to five, and ten, and then fifteen. The wind was howling outside and it was getting much colder. Buck whined and I patted his head. I stood at the door, worrying and watching for Erik through the window. I was at the point of going to get my coat and look for him when he came back with a second load of firewood.

I yanked open the door. "Are you all right? You were gone way too long."

"I'm fine," he called back. "I was checking to make sure the power lines weren't down around the house."

"In the dark, in a snowstorm?" I planted my hands on my hips. "The day after we were stalked by the cryptid?"

Erik began to unload the second round of firewood. "I had a flashlight."

"Fat lot of good that would've done you." I took two logs from him and stacked them beside the first load.

"I also had my gun on me."

I yanked a log from his hands. "Well, you could have told me that."

"Were you worried about me?" he asked as we unloaded the firewood.

"Only inasmuch that I wouldn't want to be the one to tell your folks you were attacked because you were stupid."

Buck barked in agreement.

The second batch of logs was now stacked, and he stepped in and shut the door. "The temperature is dropping fast." He tried to unzip his coat, fumbled with the zipper, and tried again.

Out of patience, I grabbed him by the elbow. "Let me." I unzipped his coat for him and tugged the coat from his arms. "Go. Sit by the fire and get warm."

"I need to take off my boots, otherwise I'll track snow through the house," he protested.

"Stomp them off the best you can, and I'll grab a towel and wipe up the hardwood floor. Don't worry about it. Go warm up."

He did as I said, and I took the towel I'd used on the dog and followed behind him, wiping up the bits of snow from his boots. Once that was finished, I returned to the mud room and stacked several logs in my arms and carried them into the living room.

As soon as he saw me walk in, he jumped to his feet.

"Oh for the love of god, McBriar," I groused. "Sit your ass down. I can carry a few logs."

I ignored his outstretched hands and deliberately walked around him to place the logs one by one in a big, sturdy basket to the left of the hearth.

"Why are you so bent out of shape?" He wanted to know.

"Because I was worried," I said. "We saw the cryptid only twenty-four hours ago, and I don't know about you, but last night made a hell of an impression on me." I stopped talking, horrified at my unintended double entendre, and placed the last remaining logs in the basket as if the fate of the world depended on their location

"I remember last night very well," he said, sitting on the brick hearth and holding his hands toward the flames.

I narrowed my eyes. "You sure don't act like it."

"We never had a chance to talk about last night."

"No, we didn't," I said. "After the police arrived it was crazy."

"I wasn't talking about the monster." He patted the spot next to him.

I sat beside him on the hearth. "What are you talking about, then?"

"I was talking about *this*," he said, and then he kissed me.

We sat before the fireplace and were lost in the kiss. While the storm raged outside, we explored each other's mouths. I ran my fingers through his short blonde hair, down to the collar of his shirt and pulled him closer. He cupped his hands under my jaw and held my face gently as our kiss continued. With a happy moan I pressed myself closer and the kiss changed. I felt the shift, and the difference in him, and I welcomed it. A moment later, when he slid his hand under my sweater, he encountered the barrier of thermal underwear… it snapped the both of us back to reality.

We both stopped and eased apart. After several humming seconds I broke the silence. "What are we doing? We don't even like each other—not really."

Erik's voice was low. "I *like* you, Ivy."

I waved his words away. "I'm not sure if you do. I'm just different. You're simply fascinated by the unknown, that's all."

"You might be magick but you don't know everything," he said. "Trust me when I say I know the difference between desire that is created by someone's magick, and the desire that is natural between two people. Like you and me."

"Well, I—" whatever else I would have said was cut off when he brushed the hair back from my face.

"I want you, Ivy," he said. "And that has nothing to do with magick and everything to do with you."

I smiled. "That's the nicest thing you've ever said to me, McBriar."

He kissed my forehead "Call me Erik."

"Erik." I gave his hand a squeeze. "So where does this leave us now?"

He studied my face carefully before he spoke. "I think it might be for the best if we get to know each other a little better."

"Yeah." I nodded. "I generally prefer to know a person fairly well before I commit to having sex."

He chuckled. "Well, that's blunt."

I gave him a friendly hip bump. "I'd rather be upfront now. Honesty today, saves from hurt feelings in the future."

He seemed to think that over as we sat side by side. "So, cards on the table?"

"You betcha," I said.

"Okay, I'll go first." He shifted closer to me. "I haven't been in a relationship since I called off my wedding a couple years ago."

"No hook-ups since then either?"

He seemed to be a tad embarrassed. "Er... no. That's not my style."

"So you're old fashioned?"

Erik shrugged. "I'd prefer to think of it as *selective*."

"Well, that's not a bad thing." I nudged him with my elbow since he was being so serious. "As for me, I ended a relationship about seven months ago. We sort of grew apart. That, and he moved back to Massachusetts for a job, after he got his degree."

"Was it hard?" Erik asked.

"No. We managed to keep things amicable. Nathan and I are friends now."

"That's nice," he said it sincerely.

"Nathan *is* a nice guy. We weren't end game, though." I shrugged.

Erik tilted his head. "End game?"

"Yeah, you know. The love of your life. Happy ever after, riding off into the sunset. Buying an old Victorian house with a big black wrought iron fence. All that sort of stuff."

"I noticed you didn't say, buying a cottage with a white picket fence." Erik smiled.

"Hello, have we met?" I cocked my head to one side. "I'd want a house with history, atmosphere and some *character.* But no matter what, I'd definitely add a fancy and gothic black iron fence to enclose the yard and garden."

"Your family home in town has a decorative fence like that. Is that why you'd want one for your own?"

"Yeah, that, and so the pets and any future babies would have a safe place to run around and play."

"Oh, so you'd want kids?"

"Well of course I'd like to have kids someday. A big goofy dog and a cat too. Kids are chaotic, messy and fun. They'd keep life from ever being boring."

"Somehow, Ivy, I doubt your future life would ever be boring."

"Wow." I pressed a hand to my heart as if overcome. "Two compliments in one evening. Maybe you do actually like me."

"Also," he began, "I should point out that I'm not the *only* one of us who is old fashioned. Miss—has her future all mapped out with house plans, pets, and babies."

"Just because I'm a Witch doesn't mean that I don't have traditional family values. Marriage, a home, and a family. There's nothing wrong with that."

"No there's not." Erik got up to poke at the logs.

The dog came over and pressed his nose to my legs. I gave him a good scratching and he sat in front of me. "I guess we'll have to sleep down here in front of the fire tonight, since the power is out."

Erik closed the mesh screen, and replaced the fireplace tongs. "The living room will definitely be the warmest room in the house."

I eyeballed the sectional. "I suppose we could sleep on opposite sides of the sectional."

Erik tucked his hands in his pockets. "We could."

"Or we could cuddle up together, and share our body heat," I said, watching for his reaction to my words. "If you are okay with simply cuddling."

"That sounds nice, actually." Erik nodded. "I'll go get some blankets."

***

I woke up because I needed to pee, and it

took me a moment to work out where I was. My face was freezing but the rest of me was warm and toasty. With a start, I remembered.

The farmhouse.

The snowstorm.

I'd slept in my thermal underwear and socks, but the flannel covered arms I was currently snuggling in belonged to none other than Erik McBriar.

Erik and I had curled up on the end of the couch closest to the fire. Currently, my back was spooned up against his chest and we were under several quilts, while the dog sprawled across our feet. I squinted in the half-light of pre-dawn and realized that my face was cold because the power was still out and the fire had died.

I lifted the blankets and eased off the side of the couch. The bathroom trip could wait. This could not. Going directly to the fireplace I gave the remnants of the fire a good poke with the tongs and added a smaller log. The coals were still hot, and it wouldn't take long for a fire to start back up. I stayed where I was, kneeling on the hearth, patiently blowing on the embers and waiting for them to flame. After they did, I added a second log to the fire. Once I was satisfied that it would stay lit, I eased back, shut the mesh screen and discovered that Erik was watching me.

"Morning," I said.

"You built that fire up nicely."

I brushed my hair back. "Babe, I got mad skills."

"Undoubtedly." He smiled and lifted the quilts. "Get back in here."

"Nature calls," I said and scurried across the living room to the first-floor bath. By the time I came back, Erik was lounging in a more upright position. When he lifted the covers, I jumped right in and pulled the blankets over my head.

"Brrr!" I shuddered, and burrowed closer. "It's nippy in here."

He tucked my head under his chin and wrapped his arms tight around me. "I'll warm you up."

"You're such a gentleman," I said, my voice muffled.

"It's the least I could do since you restarted the fire."

"What time is it?" I asked.

He checked his watch. "Six o'clock."

"Jeez! I can't believe I woke up so early." I shivered and wriggled closer. "Mmm, you're nice and warm."

"Ah, Ivy..." Erik's voice sounded funny.

"What?" I pressed tighter against him.

"Can you stop wriggling around?"

"I'm cold!"

"Yeah well, if you keep that up, we may have a bigger problem on our hands."

We were both wearing thermal underwear and he did have a flannel shirt on as well. But as I settled more firmly against him, I had no doubt as to what the 'problem' was. I pulled the blankets down to my chin so that I could see his face. "Wake up 'happy' do you?"

He swore.

"Now, now..." I patted his face. "Perhaps If you thought about something else."

He leaned his head back against the couch and chuckled.

"I could take off my socks and put my cold feet on your legs," I suggested brightly. "Bet that'd cool you off."

He burst out laughing.

"We could talk about tractors," I suggested next. "I always preferred the John Deere brand, myself."

That made him laugh even harder. "It's safe to say I've never laughed with a hard-on before."

"Stick with me, kid," I said. "You'll have all sorts of new experiences."

He groaned. "Damn it, Ivy. That is *not* helping." Erik set me aside and climbed off the couch. "I'm going to let the dog out and go make breakfast."

"If you have any soda with caffeine, you'll be my hero," I called after him as he hustled into the kitchen with Buck hot on his heels.

***

We had cold cereal and bread that we'd toasted over the fire for breakfast. Afterwards, I volunteered to do clean up while Erik started the snow blower. He geared up in coveralls and his heavy farm coat before heading out. While I still had juice in my phone, I got online to see how long the power company expected it would be before service was restored.

I called home to check on the family and discovered that they had power in town. I assured them I was fine and, depending on how soon the crews could clear out the roads, that I'd be home later in the afternoon, probably.

I studied the cozy nest that we'd made in front of the fire and was in no hurry to leave. Sure, the sexual tension made things a bit tricky, but it also made it fun. I had a sudden insight that Erik McBriar, grumpy and gorgeous though he may be, probably hadn't had much of an opportunity for fun.

He'd been working hard for the past few years to keep his family farm going. In this current economy, farmers needed to be smart and clever. Between the sales of flowers in the spring, fruit and veggies in the summer, and their pumpkin crop in the fall, they'd managed to hold onto the land.

The wedding barn venue hadn't turned out as well as they'd anticipated, but there was hope. I knew it had taken years of cultivation and planning to get to where they currently were with the Christmas tree fields, but it seemed to me that holiday sales were good.

Yes, Erik McBriar needed some laughter and fun in his life, and maybe even a bit of magick. Which made me wonder, if fate was booting me in the ass to ensure that *I* would be the one to help him find it.

CHAPTER TWELVE

It took a full day for William's Ford to dig out from ten inches of snow. However, the snow was a gorgeous and very festive addition for the third week of December. Sales were booming on Main Street, and I worked several morning shifts at *Enchantments*. Holly filled in for my evening hours that I was scheduled to be at the tree farm, but the mad rush was over for Christmas tree sales.

As Erik's parents had first explained to me, the bulk of their seasonal business hit between the weekend after Thanksgiving and up to the second weekend of December. The closer we drew to the holidays, the less folks were buying live trees. After that second weekend it was folks looking for a bargain, or simply wanting to take in the sights.

I still had plenty of clients wanting a mini holiday photo session. I did my best to steer them inside of *Mistletoe Mercantile* to pick up a few goodies before they went home. More often than not they came out with fresh greenery, a rustic holiday sign, an antique, or a Christmas ornament.

Wisely, the McBriars had shifted their focus from tree sales during the third week of December and were offering winter tractor rides and holiday workshops. Classes such as cookie decorating, ornament making, fresh wreath decorating, and so forth.

It seemed to me that they had a decent turnout, even though Erik said it was not as large as they'd hoped for. I did, however, roam around and take pictures for them to use on their website to help promote this year's and, hopefully, *next* year's holiday season.

Since he wasn't always in the tree fields now, I was able to spend more time with Erik. There wouldn't be any real opportunities for an actual date until after the holidays. But still, he was always there waiting for me when I arrived at the farm, and he also walked me to my car every evening and kissed me goodnight. The new dynamic hadn't gone unnoticed by the staff or his family. His parents hadn't said anything directly, they just gave me big smiles.

For the last big hurrah before the twenty-fifth, the McBriars had advertised for live music and a bonfire, with a gingerbread house workshop and cookie decorating at the wedding barn. The event was happening on the evening before the winter solstice, and they had high hopes for a good turnout.

I cruised up the lane to the wedding barn, and was surprised when I realized that I felt slightly depressed. After tonight, my time as the holiday photographer at the farm would be over. I parked at the far end of the parking lot and walked in, hauling my equipment and purse.

I'd barely cleared the entrance when I was greeted by Ezra. He showed me to the office where I could put my things. I hung up my coat and was lifting my camera out of the case when Erik walked in, closing the door behind him.

He leaned against the door. "It's getting crazy out there."

"Are you all ready for the big night?" I asked, looping the camera around my neck.

"As ready as we'll ever be," he said with a smile. "You look pretty tonight." He pushed away from the door, leaned down, and gave me a quick kiss. "I like that shirt."

I glanced down at my outfit. Tonight I'd worn heavy black boots, denim leggings, a red turtleneck and my red and black buffalo plaid flannel duster. "I think your penchant for flannel is starting to rub off on me, McBriar."

"I was thinking your fashion sense was starting to rub off on me as well." He held out his arms so I could take in his outfit. He was wearing dark jeans and a burgundy Henley shirt with a heavy black denim shirt over it as a jacket.

"Is that a *black* shirt?" I pressed a hand to my chest. "Be still my heart."

"It is," he said soberly. "My sister informs me that burgundy and black makes my eyes look bluer."

"Wowsers," I breathed. "Your sister is right."

The corners of his lips curved up slightly. "I thought you'd like it."

"How am I supposed to pay attention and do my job when you're gonna be walking around looking all studly and working the gothic farmer look?"

He smiled and tugged me close. "Kiss me."

"Well if you insist." I went up on my toes and kissed him, again.

We reluctantly ended the kiss because we both knew we had to get to work. I reached up and wiped my lipstick from his mouth.

"Leave it," he said.

"Your staff may start to wonder about you if you are walking around with red lipstick on…"

"Well there is that." He took a bandana from his back pocket and wiped his mouth, then he wiped a smear from my bottom lip. The gesture, although casually made, was strangely intimate. My stomach clenched hard, and I told myself to calm down and focus on the task at hand. Which was photographing the final Christmas event of the season at the farm.

"What else is there to do before opening?" I asked him.

"We already have the bonfire stacked and ready to light. Mom, Dad, Ginny and Grandma have been working their butts off all day to get ready for this event..." his voice trailed off.

I gave his hand a squeeze. "What's wrong?"

"We've had a pretty good season with tree and greenery sales. The gift shop has done very well, but the turnout for the Christmas workshops wasn't as high as I'd hoped."

"It's the night before the winter solstice, and a Friday. I bet you'll get a better turnout that you thought."

"You think so?"

"Trust me." I reached up on my toes and pressed my cheek to his. "I have a feeling."

He took my hand, and together we walked out into the main space. The barn was lit by dozens of strings of party lights and white twinkle lights. Swaths of sheer tulle were draped from the center of the high ceiling, and they formed a sort of canopy over the room. Off to the far side, a ten-foot live tree stood, it too was draped in white lights and decorated with home made ornaments.

I went over for a closer look at the tree and discovered dried orange slices on ribbons, gingerbread men, and strings of cranberries and popcorn. There were pinecones decorated with glue and glitter, obviously crafted by a child's hand. There were tiny twig stars, and red bows had been tied on various branches throughout. The tree was rustic, and absolutely charming.

I knelt, keeping the outer branches of the tree in the frame, and took several shots of the tables all with their LED candle lanterns. Diane and Ginny had tucked fresh evergreen boughs around the lanterns, and scattered pinecones around that. The décor was on point for a country farmhouse holiday, and as I straightened, a team of helpers began to set out the components for the gingerbread house and cookie decorating.

The staff was racing around, and Erik's nieces were chasing each other back and forth while their little brother toddled. I decided my best place to begin my photographs would be out of the way, and close to the main doors.

The event started right on time at seven o'clock as a few folks began to trickle in. Above the main floor, up in the loft, the musicians began to play Christmas carols. The fiddle and guitar sounded wonderful. I wandered about looking for good shots and after a while, I noticed Erik was standing alone by the front doors. He was looking miserably nervous, so I went to him and slipped my hand in his.

"There are a few more cars parking now," he said.

My instincts began to hum, and I knew at that moment that tonight would be a turning point for the farm. I was about to tell him so he wouldn't worry so much when I heard my name being called.

I saw that Bran, Lexie and their kids were walking toward the barn. "Hey, guys!" I smiled. "What are you doing here?"

"Morgan wanted to build a gingerbread house," Lexie said.

"Cookies!" Belinda yelled, happily.

I started to reply when I noticed that other familiar faces were walking forward. Autumn and Duncan had arrived. Maggie and Wyatt were walking a few feet behind them, the Vasquez family were here as well, and bringing up the rear of the group was Thomas Drake and Willow.

Most of my family had showed up to the farm, and there I was holding hands with Erik McBriar.

Nothing to do but brazen it out, I decided.

I gave Erik's hand a squeeze. "Bran, Lexie," I smiled. "This is Erik McBriar. Erik, meet my brother and sister-in-law."

"Nice to meet you," Lexie directed her comment to him, but grinned at me.

"Hello," Bran said. He didn't offer his hand because he was carrying a bundled-up Belinda.

"Hi," Erik said smoothly. "Welcome to the farm."

"Hi Ivy! Hi Erik!" Morgan grinned. "Where's your dog?"

Erik rested his hand on top of Morgan's head. "He's inside the barn staying warm."

Morgan took off in search of the dog, with his parents trailing behind him, and I looked over to focus on Autumn and Duncan as they approached.

"Is your whole family here?" Erik asked under his breath.

"No," I said, giving his hand a reassuring squeeze. "Aunt Faye is traveling and Holly is working tonight."

Even as Bran and Lexie took their family inside the barn, Autumn and her husband made a beeline for us, with Maggie and Wyatt right behind them.

"Well, well." Autumn gave mine and Erik's clasped hands a significant look. "No wonder I haven't heard from you lately."

I gave her a kiss on the cheek. "Autumn, Duncan, this is Erik."

"Hello, happy holidays!" Autumn said, cheerfully.

"Nice to meet you." Erik let go of my hand to shake both of theirs. "Welcome to the farm."

"How are you feeling, Mum?" I asked Autumn.

"I'm good. A little hungry, though," she admitted.

"There are cookies and refreshments insi—" Erik began as Autumn's eyes lit up and she was off like a shot through the barn's entrance.

"She's making up for those months when nothing would stay down." Duncan shrugged and laughed. "I guess I better go and keep an eye on her."

"Aw, give her a break," I said. "She's eating for three, after all."

"Three?" Erik asked.

"We're having twins in the spring," Duncan smiled. "I'll catch up with you later, Ivy. Nice to meet you, Erik," he said, and went inside.

I smiled as Maggie and Wyatt approached. "Hi Maggie, this is a nice surprise."

"Hey, ya'll." Maggie was wearing a long red wool coat and walking arm-in-arm with Wyatt Hastings. "I had the evening off so, we thought we'd come out tonight and enjoy the bonfire and gingerbread house making."

I waved at Nina, Diego and their baby girl, Isabel. Nina waved in return and they slipped inside the barn.

"Merry Christmas, Ms. Parish," Erik said formally to Maggie. "Please step right inside. We have tables all set up, and there is hot cider, or cocoa."

"It's his grandma's cocoa recipe, and it's amazing." I winked at Maggie.

I was surprised by Maggie being here at the farm. The last time she'd been at the barn it was to rescue her daughter, Willow, from a kidnapper. I wondered if this was going to be hard for her, but I discovered that Willow was smiling, looking around at everything, and talking a mile a minute.

Thomas Drake held Willow's hand and he gave me a nod in greeting.

"Mr. Drake." I nodded back.

"Well, this *is* a festive setting," he said, looking around. Thomas offered his free hand to Erik. "Hello, nice to meet you."

Erik handled the introduction much better than I thought.

"Thank you for coming," he said looking first at Thomas and then to Maggie. "We're happy to welcome you and your family to the farm."

"Hey, munchkin," I tweaked Willow's nose. "Happy Yule!"

"We're going to make a gingerbread house," Willow said with a giggle.

"Well, head right on in and go grab a spot at the tables." I pointed the way and the family moved to go into the barn.

"I can't believe they came." Erik's tone was soft and wondering as he stared after them.

"There's magick in the air at Yuletide," I said. "Lots of chances for new beginnings and starting over."

He grinned down at me. "I'm starting to believe it."

I felt a tingle and turned to check the lane that led up to the wedding barn. "Hey McBriar," I said. "How many tables do you have set up in there?"

"About a dozen more than we probably will need," he said. "Why do you ask?"

I pointed at the line of cars driving up the lane. "Because I think you're all going to be busier than you thought."

His eyes followed where I'd pointed. "Oh my god, look at all the cars." Erik was more than a little shell-shocked.

I took him by the arm and steered him inside. "Come on, let's go help your family. You've got a hit on your hands."

***

The barn was packed and the party was in full swing. I got a huge kick out of watching my family and friends enjoy themselves. Morgan smeared more icing on the table than he did on the gingerbread house and cookies, and Willow meticulously added every piece of candy with precision.

Autumn and Duncan were decorating a gingerbread house and debating on the cookie trees in the landscape. Lexie was keeping an eye on Belinda who was more interested in the big tree and the lights, and Diego and Nina tried to keep Isabel from eating all the candy instead of decorating her cookies with it.

After a while I put my coat back on, slipped outside to enjoy the big bonfire, and tried for some candid shots. I was surprised to discover Thomas Drake sitting on a quilt-covered hay bale and chatting up Grandma Larson. Erik, who was tending the bonfire, was standing with them and appeared to also be included in their conversation.

First off, the fact that Thomas Drake was sitting on a hay bale simply had to be documented for posterity. I snapped away and tried not to chortle with glee. As I moved around them, I happened to catch what they were saying.

"Your grandfather, Sven, was part of the group that originally searched for the creature in '79," Thomas was saying.

Erik smiled politely. "I wasn't aware my grandfather knew your family."

"Your grandfather was a gifted man," Thomas said. "He was a valued member of the council."

"Like a city council?" Erik asked and added another log to the bonfire.

Oh boy, I thought and practically tripped over my own feet in surprise. *I had to hear the rest of this conversation.*

"The creature that was first spotted by Stephen Waterman in December of 1979," Thomas said, sipping on hot cider, "was encountered again by four teens a few weeks ago."

"I was there that night." Erik nodded. "I heard the yelling and went to help those kids."

"You were there, because you were tracking what you imagined to be an animal that killed one of the farm dogs," his grandmother pointed out. "But, Erik, it wasn't a coyote, or a bobcat."

"Are you saying you think it was a bear?" Erik asked.

"Did you see anything that night in November?" Thomas asked him. "Anything you couldn't explain?"

Erik stopped tending the fire and studied Thomas. "No, but Ivy and I saw something very strange, last week out in the tree fields."

"Do you know what it was?" Thomas asked.

"I have absolutely no idea what kind of creature—animal it was."

"I do," Grandma Larson said.

"Did you see something that night too, Grandma?" Erik sounded alarmed. "Why didn't you say anything?"

"What you saw was a creature from the *vild jagt*—the wild hunt."

Erik smiled indulgently. "Grandma, I know that you love to tell old Scandinavian folk tales..."

Greta made a sharp motion with her hand. "You will listen to me, Erik! This is no folk tale! The Allfather has been roaming the forest and the fields trying to gather up the lost creatures from the hunt. I have seen him, myself."

"The Allfather?" Erik frowned. "Why does that sound so familiar?"

"Because," she said, "you are remembering the stories I told you about Odin when you were small."

"In Norse mythology," Thomas began, "Odin hung on Yggdrasil, the world tree, for nine days in order to discover the Runes."

I joined the three of them, placing my hand on Greta's shoulder. "Did I hear you say that you've seen Odin? Here on the farm?"

"I have," she said firmly.

"What did he look like?" I couldn't resist asking.

"His hair and beard were long, wild and gray," Greta began, "he wore a long, hooded, fur trimmed jacket—"

"With tall handmade looking boots, leather pants and a linen shirt?" I interrupted her.

"Yes." She nodded.

"Was he sort of lean and athletic, appeared to be in his mid-fifties?"

"Yes, *min lille heks*. He did."

"That sounds like the same guy I met in the

woods, when I was out looking around the park after the attack."

"When was this?" Erik demanded.

"Weeks ago." I shook my head. "I thought he was a Renaissance Faire cast member trying out his costume, but there was something about him. I remember he spooked me because he knew my name." I started to laugh in wonder. "No wonder he seemed almost paternal!"

"Ivy!" Erik sounded horrified.

I waved that off, and gave my attention to his grandmother. "When the man left he said something to me… it sounded like *flare-lee yule*."

"*Glædelig Jul,*" Greta said.

I pointed. "That's it exactly. What does it mean?"

She smiled, beautifully. "It means, 'Merry Christmas', or more correctly, 'Merry Yule', in Danish."

"So we have a guy creeping around the area in costume and he speaks Danish?" Erik folded his arms over his chest. "Is that what you're telling me?"

"No." Greta rose to her feet and stared down

her grandson. "I am telling you that the god of my ancestors, *your* ancestors, has answered my call and has come to protect us."

Erik did a double take. "Answered your prayers?"

"Erik." I took his hand. "Don't you understand?" Before I could say anything else, Thomas Drake chimed in.

"Your grandfather was a mage." Thomas' voice was quiet but serious as he addressed Erik. "Sven Larson was powerful. I knew him when I was a young man, and was honored to have been accepted as his student."

"My grandfather *taught* you?" Erik shook his head. "That's ridiculous! He was a farmer, and you're an estate lawyer or some type of real estate broker. What could you two possibly have in common?"

"Magick," I said. "Erik, you need to connect the dots. Your grandfather wasn't on a *city* council."

"Grandma?" Erik looked to Greta for confirmation.

"Your grandfather *was* a mage," she said. "He was a talented, complex man, and he did take on students. He taught both Ivy's mother, *and* Thomas here, rune-craft when they were young."

That bit of information had me reeling. I hadn't known my mother had ever been a pupil of Sven Larson's. *How cool was that?*

"Does my mother know about any of this?" Erik asked, incredulously.

"Diane has chosen *not* to know," Greta said with a nod.

"I see," Erik said slowly. "And am I to assume that you know so much about Norse mythology because of Grandpa?"

"Erik," I gave his arm a gentle squeeze. "What part of her saying, 'I called upon the gods of my ancestors,' did you not understand?"

"So you're Pagan?" His voice was shaky and unsure as he addressed his grandmother.

Thomas rose to his feet. "I understand that you aren't comfortable with the idea of magick, or the old religion. However, the truth of it is all around you. You are not merely a spectator from the outside, young man."

"I'm starting to get that." Erik rubbed his

forehead. "It's just a lot to take in."

Greta stayed where she was, and in the flickering light from the bonfire, wearing a dark hooded coat, she appeared every bit the wise Crone. "This is your heritage and your grandfather's legacy, we are talking about," she said to her grandson. "On this midwinter's night you were told the truth. How you choose to go forward, and what you decide to do with this information is up to you."

Erik nodded to his grandmother. "Thank you for telling me the truth."

"If you wish to speak to me more about this, come and find me later," Greta said.

"I better tend to the fire." Erik stepped back and walked away.

I stood there with Greta and Thomas and watched as he moved to the far side of the bonfire and began to add a few more logs.

"That honestly went better than I expected," Thomas said.

Greta sighed. "He will brood over this for a few days. Mark my words."

"I guess I better go talk to him," I said.

Greta smiled. "I'm glad that he has you."

I inclined my head to Thomas and Greta and walked over to Erik. "Hey," I said after a moment.

"Hey," he glanced at me and then returned his attention to the fire.

"I'm here," I said. "If you want, or need to talk."

"This has been a great night!" An attendee clapped Erik on the shoulder. "We'll definitely come back next year."

Erik smiled at the man and wished him a good night. But afterward, when he shifted back to me, the smile struck me as forced and false.

"Erik?" I reached for his hand.

"I only want to know one thing."

My stomach dropped. Erik might be standing there smiling pleasantly for the crowd, but inside he was angry and upset. "What did you want to know?" I asked.

He shifted closer to me so he wouldn't be overheard. "Did you know about my grandparents all along?"

"No," I said, gently squeezing his hand. "I found out about your grandfather a couple weeks ago. Back when Thomas told me about the original group of men who went searching for the creature in '79. And believe me, I was shocked."

"And my grandmother? Did you know about her too?"

"I suspected, but wasn't absolutely sure until the night of the full moon."

"And you didn't think to share that information with me?" Erik's facial expression was pleasant, but his tone was not.

I kept my voice low and tried to stay calm. "It was certainly not my place to 'out' your grandparents, Erik."

"I'm going to need some time," he said. "Time to let this sink in."

"Of course."

He looked pointedly at my hand. "I'm going to need some space as well."

I let go of his hand immediately. "You want space?" I stepped back. "You got it."

"Ivy, I..." he trailed off. The emotions radiating off him were hurt, anger, and disbelief. "I need to get more wood for the fire," he decided. "Excuse me."

He walked off and I let him go. While people laughed and chatted around me, I felt a deep disappointment. Here I'd thought he was loosening up a bit, but clearly this had been too much for him. With a frustrated sigh, I realized that Erik was going to have to come to terms with the reality of his heritage on his own.

People were starting to leave the event and there was no need for me to remain any longer. I slipped back inside, gathered up my camera bag and packed up. I wished everyone a happy holiday and slipped out with a large group of attendees. I walked silently to my car and started it.

I clicked on the radio, and Mariah Carey's, *All I Want For Christmas Is You*, blasted out of the car speakers. I rolled my eyes to the heavens. "Thanks for that. Oh, cruel and heartless Yuletide gods." The last thing I needed was to hear that manic song right now.

I switched the channel and *Blue Christmas* by Kelly Clarkson was playing. I dropped my head to the steering wheel and began to laugh.

I backed out of the parking space and rolled along with the traffic as we made our way down the long gravel drive. Tomorrow was the solstice, and my family would be exchanging gifts in the morning, and then having an afternoon feast. I told myself not to mope, and instead to focus on the fun of the family celebrations and the coming holiday festivities over the next few days.

"I'll miss this place," I admitted as I drove out the main gates for the final time and pulled onto the highway. I sighed, and even as I fought it, one tear managed to escape. I wiped it away immediately. There was absolutely no reason to let Erik McBriar ruin my holidays.

He wasn't my boyfriend, we weren't even dating. Not really. This had been a job-place flirtation, and nothing more. I squared my shoulders and told myself to look back at the few weeks I'd spent at the farm as a pleasant and profitable time for myself, and my photography career.

The song switched to a version of *The Holly and the Ivy*, and determined to be cheerful, I sang along with the carol on my way back into William's Ford.

CHAPTER THIRTEEN

The winter holidays sped by. The morning of the solstice was a blast with Belinda and Morgan tearing into their presents with glee. Bran, Lexie, Holly, Autumn, Duncan and I had all exchanged our gifts that morning as well. Aunt Faye face timed us from Greece and informed us that she and Dr. Meyer had gotten married. Which only added to the craziness and happiness.

I got a fabulous surprise when I discovered that my family had all gone in together and bought me a softbox umbrella lighting kit for my photography business. I had been set up to rent one for formal portraits at Violet and Matthew's wedding. But now I had my very own. I was beyond excited to try it out and see what I could do with it.

On Christmas Eve we'd all been invited to the Drake's house for a fancy dinner party, and it was fun getting all dressed up and hanging out with Maggie, Wyatt and Willow, the Vasquez family and even Thomas and Julian Drake.

Thomas bought an extravagant double baby stroller for Autumn and Duncan and their forthcoming twins. My cousin cried when she opened the present and saw it. He had gifts for everyone else too, and I was touched when he passed on a set of handmade Runes to me, explaining that they had once belonged to my mother.

It was a glittering and elegant evening, and it felt like stepping into another world. I never expected to have so much fun, but we all did. After the food, everyone played board games and cards.

I'd sat elbow to elbow with Diego and Wyatt, while Bran, Thomas, Julian and Duncan sat around the table, playing poker. The seven of us had played cards and after an hour, it was clear that no one could beat Julian. That is until

Holly sat in to play a few hands. Then he started to lose every time. To Holly.

The children all ran around the mansion, Lexie and Autumn sat and talked babies with Nina and Maggie, and I tried not to think about Erik, or what he was doing.

Enchantments opened back up the day after Christmas and it was my turn to work. We didn't have many exchanges, but we did get a lot of business from gift certificates. Holly asked if I could take her shifts over the weekend as she had an opportunity to go on a business trip with the museum.

She was pretty excited about it, and I wondered if she was dating someone from work, or maybe a grad student who volunteered at the museum. I didn't push her on it and told her I was happy to help, as she had filled in for me while I'd been busy with all the seasonal photography at the tree farm.

I could privately admit to being down in the dumps after everything that had and *hadn't* happened with Erik. But I was determined not to let it show. On the last Saturday of December, I decided to cheer myself up by dressing my witchiest, and was wearing a long black broomstick skirt, a black sweater and a burgundy lace shawl tied over that.

I'd added my big silver pentagram that my mother had given me when I was a teen and had done my makeup in deep purples and burgundy. I'd added a black eye liner, drawing a thick cat eye. I slicked on some blood red lipstick and wore my raw ruby crystal point earrings. I had stopped playing the holiday music in the shop —it was getting on my last nerve—and instead was playing classic Fleetwood Mac and Stevie Nicks music.

The group had been one of my mother's favorite bands, and the music was comforting. While it sounded through the store's speakers, I tried to keep my mind occupied, and tackled the re-alphabetizing of the non-fiction books on the store's shelves. I'd pulled all the out of order books, stacking them in one arm, and was putting them in their proper places, when a large book fell off the shelf and bopped me on the head.

"Ouch!" I laughed and rubbed my head. I bent over to pick up the book and discovered it was a volume on the Norse gods. "Very funny," I groused, as I shoved it back into place.

The bells above the doors chimed. I glanced casually over my shoulder and almost bobbled all the books I held.

Erik McBriar had just walked into our store.

He was looking sharper than I'd ever seen him. Black jeans, dark boots, and a stylish fleece-lined leather bomber jacket. *Aw, hell,* I thought. *Did he have to look so damn good?*

"Hello, Erik," I said, as calmly as possible. "What brings you here today?"

"Ivy?" he blinked at me as he stood in the open door.

I smirked. "In the flesh."

"Whoa, you look different."

I skimmed a hand down over the skirt. "Actually, this is the *real* me."

"It's a different look than what I'm used to," he said.

The shop's door closed firmly behind him, causing Erik to jump in surprise. I took a deep breath, reigned my power back in, and reminded myself that a wise practitioner kept control over her emotions.

He stepped forward and smiled. "Do you always dress up like this when you work at the store?"

Dress up? I thought, and was surprised that the comment had hurt my feelings. "Are you insinuating that I'm wearing a *costume*?"

"No," he said. "I've never seen you looking so witchy, before."

I deliberately set the books down on one of the chairs in the reading section. "Did you drop by just so you could make fun of me?"

"Of course not! The style of clothing you wear makes no difference to me."

"Well there's a relief," I snarked.

"I figured that you might be mad after the other night—"

"Honestly, I'm *disappointed* in you," I cut him off. "I always knew you were prejudiced against Witches and Pagans but I'd truly hoped that after we'd become...friends...that your perception had shifted and that your opinions had changed."

"You think I'm prejudiced?"

"I *know* you are." I crossed my arms over my chest. "Bigotry toward another person's religion, is as bad as being intolerant because of someone's ethnicity."

"I am *not* a bigot," Erik said, firmly. "I will admit that I'm still working on being comfortable with the whole witchcraft thing. That's a hard one for me."

"Then what in the sweet hell were you doing kissing me?" I demanded. "Were you bored and decided to take a walk on the wild side, McBriar?"

"That's not fair," he said. "I'm trying to be honest with you. And as to your clothes, while it may have caught me a little off-guard to see you in a long dress—"

"It's a *skirt*." I corrected him.

"Skirt." He nodded. "My mistake."

"This is how I typically dress, when I'm not working as a photographer," I said. "I prefer dark colors, and romantic gothic styles."

"At the farm you always wore practical, normal clothes." He shrugged. "I suppose I figured that's how you always dressed."

"*Normal* clothes?" My eyes narrowed. "Are you trying to be insulting, or are you really that damn clueless?" I felt the energy shift a second before I saw that the stack of books on the chair beside me were all starting to hover.

A wise practitioner avoids public or unnecessary displays of power, I tried to recite my mantra and find inner peace...

But, fuck it. I was boiling mad.

I pointed at one of the nearby books and sent it flying across the room straight at his thick skull.

He yelped and barely managed to avoid getting beaned with the book. He wasn't so lucky with the second, or the third book I sent flying his way. The oversized paperbacks hit his chest with very satisfactory smacks.

"Hey! Hey! Take it easy!" He held up his hands in surrender. "I didn't come here to fight with you over fashion! I wanted to apologize."

"You're apologies *suck,* McBriar." I pointed, and a fourth rose up.

"I'm sorry!" he said. "I'm sorry for the way I acted the night of the bonfire. I was sort of shell-shocked, I guess."

"Go on," I said. "I'm listening."

"You gonna nail me with that book too?"

"No, I think I've made my point." I focused

and the book dropped back to the chair.

Erik let out a careful breath. "You were trying to be supportive and kind that night, and I shut you out because I was upset." He bent over to gather the paperbacks I'd sent flying at him. He scooped them off the floor, walked over to me, and held them out. "I'm sorry again for my behavior, Ivy. It wasn't fair to you. Not at all."

I kept my mouth shut, took the books, and shoved them back on the shelf before I said or did anything else rash.

"After what I found out at the bonfire," Erik said, "I needed some time to let everything sink in."

"Well, how lovely. I hope you had a delightful holiday *alone* with your thoughts."

"Not especially." He tucked his hands in his jacket pockets. "Everything I thought I knew about myself was basically stripped away."

"And people accuse me of being dramatic," I grumbled.

"What was that?" he asked.

I tossed up my hands. "For goddess sake! You found out your maternal grandparents were a different religion, and you had yourself a snit because the truth ruined your perfectly Protestant, homogenized world."

"Homogenized?" Erik tilted his head. "Did you just insult me with a farming analogy?"

"Oh, grow the fuck up McBriar," I snapped.

"Hold on," he said, taking my hand. "I said that I came here because I wanted to talk to you—and I do."

"Well tragically, I have no time to spare." I made a shooing gesture with my free hand. "Run along now, like a good little farm boy and don't let the door hit you in the ass on your way out."

Instead of stomping off like I'd imagined, he smiled. "You really are beautiful."

I swallowed hard, and took a cautious step back from him and the compliment. "Get lost, Erik. I have work to do." He wasn't reacting in any way that I'd come to anticipate and I grabbed the remaining books on the chair. Hoping to appear indifferent, I tried to reshelf a few titles, but my hands were shaking and I dropped one.

"You're acting very nervous all of the

sudden." He sounded pleased at the discovery and a slow smile spread across his face.

"You're delusional." I tossed my head. "Leave, before I turn you into a frog."

"Nope," he said. "You told me yourself, harming someone is against the rules."

I nailed him with my haughtiest look. "I'd be willing to make an exception in your case."

"I guess I'll have to risk it then, because I'm not going anywhere." He took the books from my arms and set them down. "I have something for you."

"What?" I asked suspiciously as he reached in his coat pocket.

He pulled out a sprig of fresh mistletoe. "You told me once this was a plant of peace. Well I did some research—"

"I hope that wasn't too much of a strain for you," I said tartly.

He kept right on talking as if I hadn't interrupted. "*and* I found out it's also associated with love and forgiveness."

"I...I..." He'd reduced me to stammering. "I don't have time for this random attempt at charm."

"It's not an attempt." He held the sprig high, and with his other arm he pulled me close.

"What do you think—" My words came out breathy and I cleared my throat. "You're doing?"

"Traditionally a kiss under the mistletoe was supposed to be magickal. I thought you of all people would appreciate that."

"It is also used in invisibility spells," I said. "I'm sure I have enough supplies here at the store to put something together to make you disappear."

"Ivy," he chuckled, and continued to simply hold me.

"Mistletoe is associated with thunder, too." I raised an eyebrow. "Care to try your luck?"

I wasn't sure when it had happened, but my arms had crept around his waist, and I was holding on to him as well. For a few moments we just stayed as we were, staring at each other.

"I missed you," we said at the same time. Then we smiled.

I went up on my toes, he bent his head down, and we kissed.

The kiss was sweet, and afterward he

lowered the mistletoe, and simply rested his forehead against mine.

His emotions crashed over me, and I sensed: regret, nervousness, loneliness, and worry. Worry that he'd screwed up any chance he might have had with me, because he was falling in love...With me.

And that was the biggest surprise of all.

He loved me.

"I'm picking up on your emotions," I explained, easing back from him. "*All* of them, especially when you hold me that close. It's, ah, not fair, me being able to read you. Especially since you don't know how to protect your private thoughts."

"Oh." He took my hand and looked carefully into my eyes. "That's the empathy thing, right?"

"For someone who isn't comfortable with the Craft, you certainly do have a decent working knowledge of it."

"I learned from the best." He gave my fingers a gentle squeeze.

I couldn't help the laugh that escaped. "Sweet talker."

"You know what?" he asked quietly.

"What?"

He handed me the mistletoe. "When you left, you took all the light with you."

"I didn't *do* anything to you—" I began.

"I wasn't implying that you had," he cut in.

"There were no spells, or—" My words caught in my throat when Erik pulled me close.

"Ivy, will you please stop rambling, shut up, and kiss me?"

"Well, I'm seriously thinking about it," I said, with our mouths only a couple inches apart.

He waited a beat. "Still thinking?"

"If you knew what I was thinking, you'd probably run for cover."

He ran a gentle hand up my back. "I'm crazy about you," he said.

"I *know*." I smiled, as we continued to stand in each other's arms.

"I figured that you might know," he said. "With the whole PK thing and your empathy."

I tucked the mistletoe behind my ear. "Did I mention I'm also an intuitive?"

Erik chuckled. "I can't remember. I was too

busy dodging paperbacks."

"Them's the breaks," I said, cheerfully. "Kiss me again, Erik."

He swooped in and I wrapped my arms around his neck and held on tight. This was the sort of kiss that had my head spinning and my belly quivering. We were standing in the middle of the sales floor, making out for the longest time, and I truly didn't care.

Things were getting intense, and I think that we both realized at the same time that there was only so far we could take this kiss. We broke apart, our breathing ragged and grinned at each other.

With a sigh, I laid my head on his chest and listened to his heart. It was racing as fast as mine.

"Ivy," he said, kissing the top of my hair. "Life was so incredibly dull without you around."

I lifted my head and smiled. "Missed my dazzling personality, did you?"

"My dad called it, *sparkle*. But it's more like magick. Your magick."

"It's a part of who I am, Erik. I won't deny

that fact, nor will I ever hide it."

"I know, and I'm glad," he said. "Do you have any idea what you did for our farm? Those photos you took of Morgan and Buck in the old red truck, they started everything. We had our best year *ever.* My parents were pretty upset with me that I hadn't invited you to Christmas dinner with the family."

"Why didn't you?" I asked.

"I had planned to, the night of the bonfire, but afterwards I was embarrassed about the way I'd reacted to everything. And I didn't want to ruin any holiday plans you might have had with *your* family."

"We don't celebrate on the twenty-fifth. I actually stayed in my attic apartment at the manor and binge-watched a series on television."

"You told me about Yule, the day I gave you the tree for your apartment. I should have remembered you celebrated then. So, did you have a good holiday with your family?"

"I did."

"Mom and Dad had a family meeting on the twenty-sixth and came up with all sorts of new ideas for next year's Christmas tree season, and the *Mistletoe Mercantile,*" he said. "They also talked about having you come back to do holiday photos, and my dad wants you to take more photographs of the wedding venue for our farm's website."

"I'd enjoy that very much. Maybe I could do a series of seasonal photos of the farm too?"

Erik nodded in agreement. "Oh and speaking of seasons, the family wants to offer you a contract for those mini-sessions for fall pumpkin picking and Halloween time. I told them that you'd probably have the best idea for Halloween photos."

I kissed him. "Your enthusiasm is kind of sexy, McBriar. I'll talk to your parents about that. I'm sure we can work something out for next fall."

"My parents are your number one fans," Erik said. "Actually, my dad took me aside on Christmas day and asked me what the hell I'd done to screw things up with you."

I smiled. "Did he?"

"He did. Then after he was finished with me, Grandma Larson whapped me up the backside of my head and told me that only a fool walks away from someone who brings magick into their life."

I laughed over that mental image. "Well, she would know."

"She lent me some old books the other day. Books that had belonged to my grandfather, and they're fascinating. I've been studying them."

"What did you learn?" I asked.

"That there's a lot more to this world than I ever thought possible. I felt a sort of connection to the nature-based stuff and the year wheel."

"Wheel of the year," I corrected.

"Yeah, that was interesting, and I like the idea of working with the energies of the seasons. I don't feel a calling to practice magick, not like he did. But I *do* respect my ancestors, and my heritage."

"I would imagine your grandfather would be content with that."

"Can *you* be content with that?" he asked.

"All I would expect out of a partner with regards to my spirituality is that they were open-minded, and accepting. I wouldn't demand that they convert. That goes against free will."

"Ivy." He took my hands in his. "I wouldn't ever want you to be anything other than who you are."

That got me. Tears began to well up in my eyes, and my heart fell. I practically heard it hit the floor with a *splat*.

I was falling in love with him. I sniffled happily at the realization and worked not to let the tears fall. I didn't want to cry, not now. But a few tears escaped anyway.

Erik wiped them away himself. "Anyway," he said gently, "now that we had this chance to talk and to clear the air. Maybe we can move forward, as a couple."

"I'd say we've made a good start," I agreed. "I don't stand around making out with every random hot farmer who walks into *Enchantments,* you know."

He dropped another quick kiss on my lips. "How do you feel about going out for dinner tonight? We're long overdue for a real date."

"I'd like that," I agreed. "What did you have in mind?"

Erik opened his mouth to reply but before he

could speak, the door opened and Eddie O'Connell walked in with a bounce in his step.

"Hey, Ivy." He waved. "Hi Erik!"

"Hello, Eddie," I said. "You seem upbeat and happy. Did you have a good holiday?"

"Yeah, Yule was great!" He grinned. "But I dropped by to tell you about what happened last Friday."

"What happened?" Erik asked the teen.

"Well, me and Caleb were visiting Hunter and this guy from the conservation department dropped by the Rolands' house."

"No kidding?" I said. "What for?"

"He came by to check on how Hunter was recovering, and to tell us that the animal that had attacked Hunter *was* a bear. He said it was deformed, and that's why it looked so weird. The agent said that he and his companions had been tracking it for weeks, but they finally found it, captured it, and had it removed from the area."

I stayed silent while Eddie continued to speak.

"Anyway, the agent asked me to pass along the information on to you and Erik too," Eddie said. "But they caught it—whatever it was—and they removed it! Isn't that great news?"

I nodded. "That is good news." *And total bullshit,* I thought. *I'd seen the thing for myself. It hadn't been a deformed bear.*

"I haven't heard from anyone at the conservation department." Erik's words pulled me from my thoughts. "Have you been contacted, Ivy?"

"Well, no, I haven't," I admitted. "I did make some calls to the local office a few weeks ago." I focused on Eddie. "I don't suppose the agent left you a way to contact him, did he?"

"Uh, yeah, he did." Eddie patted around the pockets of his coat and pulled a business card out and handed it over to me.

The card read: *AF Wodin, Wildlife and Game.*

I almost laughed out loud, but managed to keep a sober expression. I showed the card to Erik and he did a double take. "You know, Eddie," I said, trying to sound casual. "I think I might have spoken to your conservation agent, after all. What did he look like?"

"He was totally cool," Eddie said. "He had

like a flowing beard with long silver hair. He was tall and built. But even though he wore a uniform, he was the most bad-ass looking guy."

"Kind of like a Viking?" I asked.

"Yeah, totally." Eddie nodded.

"What color were his eyes?" I asked.

"Blue." Eddie shrugged. "One of them was anyway, the other was sort of white looking. I guess he had an old injury or something."

"I see." I gave Erik a sidelong look, but smiled reassuringly to Eddie.

"Anyway, I wanted to tell you the good news in person. Thanks for helping me with all of this, Ivy." Eddie smiled. "And thanks again, Erik for your help the night Hunter was hurt."

"Of course." Erik smiled.

Behind me the books I'd never finished reorganizing slid over, and one fell off the shelf.

Eddie moved to pick it up. "Hey, this book on Norse mythology looks cool. How much is it?

"It's on the house," I said, spontaneously. "I have a feeling it's a book you need to read. Consider it a holiday present."

"Really?" Eddie flipped through the pages.

"Thanks Ivy, I don't know a lot about the Norse pantheon."

"Seems to me that it's time you do," I said.

"Thanks!" Eddie smiled. "See you guys around." With a friendly wave, he headed for the door.

I waited until the door had shut and turned to Erik. "What do you think?"

Erik walked straight to the empty chair in the reading section and sat down. "That was absolutely bizarre."

"Did you know that Odin roams the earth before Yule checking on folks and spreading good will—"

"Like Santa Claus?"

"Odin was the precursor to Santa Claus," I said. "He flew around on an eight-legged horse."

Erik chuckled. "I didn't know that."

"I think your grandmother was right," I said. "I think that Odin and his *companions* have been more than a little busy in William's Ford these past few weeks."

"By companions you mean the wild hunt thing, right?" Erik asked.

"Exactly." I nodded.

"Hey, can I see that card again?" Erik asked.

"Sure." I handed it over.

"AF Wodin?" Erik frowned. "Is that a play on Odin?"

"I bet AF is for Allfather, and *Wodin* is a variation of Odin," I said. "Did you know that Wednesday, was once known as Wodin's day?"

Erik started to laugh. "Do you think it was one of those Renaissance players that visited those boys, a conservation agent, or something else?"

I dropped my hand on his shoulder and gave him a bolstering pat. "My gut tells me whoever it was, it *wasn't* an actor, or a conservation agent."

"I am going to have to agree. Did you happen to see what was written on the back of the card?" Erik flipped it over and held it up for me.

"Is that German?" I asked.

"It's Danish," Erik explained.

"So what's it say?"

"*Hav et gadt nytår*— is 'Happy New Year' in Danish," Erik said. "My grandfather used to shout that in Danish every year, when he set off fireworks at midnight."

"That sounds like fun," I said.

"It was fun." Erik grinned. "He used to try and get us to eat boiled cod too. It's a Danish thing."

I made a face. "Boiled fish sounds *nasty*."

"Trust me. It is." He stood up. "Do you have any plans for New Years Eve?"

"I promised to babysit Morgan and Belinda, so my brother and his wife could go out."

"Would you like some company?"

"Not if it involves cod." I waited a beat. "Dinner tonight better not have boiled fish, either."

Erik laughed and took my hand. "I promise, no fish."

"Well, so long as I have your word," I said, giving his hand a squeeze. "How 'bout I close up early and we get started on that first official date?"

"You can do that, just close up early?"

"Of course I can, I'm part owner." I pointed at the door and the locks flipped and the sign turned from open to closed.

"That PK thing you do is so cool," Erik said.

"McBriar..." I reached up and gave him a kiss. "You ain't seen nothing yet."

***

It didn't take long to close the shop, and afterward Erik and I went to a pub on Main Street and had a cozy dinner. We sat side-by-side splitting a pizza and a bottle of wine, talking about his future plans for the farm, my upcoming solo wedding photo gig, our families, and of course, magick.

He raised his wine glass. "*Hav et gadt nytår.*"

"Happy New Year," I said back, tapping my glass to his.

The future stretched out before us, full of possibilities and love, and I knew deep down that ours would be magickal and bright.

The End

Turn the page to discover more about the bewitching town of William's Ford as Ellen Dugan's *Legacy of Magick* series continues...

Cakepops, Charms & Do No Harm
By Ellen Dugan

Candice Jacobs is as sweet as they come. Her popular confectionary shop is a hit with the residents of William's Ford and business is booming, until a jealous baker from a nearby town drops dead on the sidewalk in front of Candice's store.

If that wasn't bad enough, a series of bizarre events begin to befall Candice. Now rumors are stirring that everyone's favorite Kitchen Witch might be dabbling in black magick. With her professional and personal reputation crumbling, Candice must figure out who or what is the cause—and she better do it fast.

Witches vow to 'do no harm', but somebody sure does want Candice and her business out of the way. Will her magick be able to save her in time?

Cakepops, Charms & Do No Harm: Book 11 in the *Legacy Of Magick* series,
coming January 2021

ABOUT THE AUTHOR

Ellen Dugan is the award-winning author of over twenty-eight books. Ellen's popular non-fiction titles have been translated into over twelve foreign languages. She branched out successfully into paranormal fiction with her popular *Legacy Of Magick, The Gypsy Chronicles,* and *Daughters Of Midnight* series. Ellen has been featured in USA TODAY'S HEA column. She lives an enchanted life in Missouri tending to her extensive perennial gardens and writing. Please visit her website and blog:

www.ellendugan.com
www.ellendugan.blogspot.com

Made in the USA
Monee, IL
22 November 2019